CLACKAMAS LITERARY REVIEW

2025
Volume XXIX

Clackamas Community College
Oregon City, Oregon

CLACKAMAS LITERARY REVIEW

Managing Editors
Ryan Davis & Matthew Warren

Associate Editors
Angela Hughes   Jennifer Pons   Nicole Rosevear

Amy Warren

Assistant Editors & Designers
Rae Barnes   Silvia Raquel Diaz Diaz   Sarah A. Grabeel

Bev N. Siefer   Mars Wright

Cover Art
Tree-lined Path by Carina Cooper

The *Clackamas Literary Review* is published annually at Clackamas Community College. Manuscripts are read from September 1st to December 31st. By submitting your work to *CLR*, you indicate your consent for us to publish accepted work in print and online. Issues I–XI are available through our website; issues XII–XXVIII are available on our Submittable, and through your favorite online bookseller.

Clackamas Literary Review
19600 Molalla Avenue, Oregon City, Oregon 97045
ISBN: 978-1-7320333-7-5
Printed by Lightning Source
www.clackamasliteraryreview.org

CONTENTS

PROSE

CONTRIBUTORS

Editors' Note

Lost in memories of a lover gone, a person stares absentmindedly into their tea, their past relationship immortalized in a story for those who know such loss. After many betrayals of a bitter sister, a woman walks headfirst into a storm she knows could end her, her inner battle written for others who also face such struggles. Children reach out for a mother who is both in front of them yet unreachable, their pain laid bare for the ones who know such pain.

Time spent together with others leaves a mark on us, reminds us of who we were. Bill Schreiber reflects on this in his poem:

I ache for a smell I don't remember

a thing I held but fell through my fingers

We all know that ache, that longing for bonds created then unmade, held close before they slipped away. And even when those memories fade, we yearn for what we felt in those moments. This year's collection is brimming with stories both reaching for, and reveling in, the connections we create with others. We hope that within these pages of the *Clackamas Literary Review* you find such belonging.

All I Want

Richard Robbins

To stand hip-deep in the ocean, waves
never breaking high enough to knock
me down. Pelicans skim along the crests—
All I want is that they pay no mind.

Those sandstone cliffs rise and recede
beyond the shore. They hold up the homes.
Down the beach, people on the pier cast out
fishing lines, walk in pairs to the end,

where they stop to look for Asia. All
I want is the wind in my hand: that
small country, yearning. All I want for homes,
the pier, for bodies speckling the sand

like jazz is that the army take down
its flag, the country dry its tears
in the music under this one sun.

How Do I Love You?

Cecil Morris

—with apologies to Elizabeth Barrett Browning

How do I love you? Let me think now. Let me think.
Not with the fence-chewing, ball-chasing, hole-digging
ardor, the panting fervor I gave my first wife
who, it turned out, preferred the calmer attentions
of an older dog. Not like that. No. And not with
the suspicious, border-patrolling vigilance
I lavished on my second wife who, it turned out,
did not care for bark or snarl or midnight howl.
No, my love for you is not that, not bluff and brag.
I love you like that warm presence stretched at your feet,
relaxed and patient attentiveness, my two ears
even in sleep attuned to your breathing, your dreams,
the range of beach or field you choose for us to roam,
and this home you make for us. That's how I love you.

Late May

Nick Conrad

There was the randomness of our witnessing
those light-struck clouds, the air feigning a frost

after early May's furnace days. It was
a week before your second CT scan. The days

spent lost in a pretense of purpose were
already long gone. The earth, sodden from the week's

torrential rain, gave under foot; the known path
a liquid slurry. To the passing neighbor,

we were just two fools gawking at the changing sky.
I doubt anyone caught your smile.

The Glissade Down Little Annapurna

Eric le Fatte

In your orbits, you carry us, as though willingly,
through the heavens on your back:
some on your snow-capped spine,
others by rivers, oceans, deserts, fields of grain.

Forgive us if we've forgotten
we are passengers, that translations
of time vary as much
as faces of the wind.

We've missed the eons of arrivals,
heydays, and vanishings you've witnessed,
and must climb above the trees
to configure all the pieces.

Today, while the present wind blows many knots,
with ridges lined up like vertebrae,
as snows of a thousand years slip beneath my feet,
the sun blinks through your eyes.

It's a steep glissade down from your shoulder.

You have me now.

I will hold on tight.

A Postcard Poem from *To Punani Camp*

samodH Porawagamage

My Fortune,

Latest gossip is that Rathu and Sarala have dug up a treasure! Both have stopped working and haven't been seen for weeks now. Villagers say they are happy for the couple, but I can hear their teeth clench in envy like fireworks. I'm sure many wish the treasure is cursed. If it's true, I'm happy for the poor couple. They have had such a tough life since Rathu lost a leg in that landmine, and they dedicated their lives into the treasure business. Let's hope they'll be careful with the money: buried treasure or lottery ticket, whoever came across a sudden fortune around here wasn't wise handling it. Your mother says the real curse is trashy mouths of the villagers. I don't want to tell her that it's human folly to lose control when there's plenty. None of this matters to me because I've found my own treasure six years ago! Just when I thought I wouldn't share a fraction of you, you gave me our precious little Niduk.

Fortune-finder

Santa Fe

Sam Spring

The prickly pear tea brought him back to Santa Fe—brought him back to her. It had been years since that week in the small adobe brick shack outside of town, nestled amongst the rolling dunes and the looming saguaros. *How long ago had it been? Seven years? Ten years?* He would have been a younger man then, just turned twenty-one and she, an older woman. She had seen decades of change in the city before he was even born. And still more before he had even stepped foot off the train into her strange land. She fascinated him—in the way she thought, in the way she spoke, in the way her strong-legged silhouette straddled him in the flicker of candlelight. He bowed to her gospel.

He had promised to return while they stood on the platform the morning of his final day in the desert. Boarding the train, he looked back to find her standing there, arms crossed, the right side of her full lips curved up in a knowing smile. He was ephemeral—a passerby, and she, a permanent fixture amongst the terracotta landscape. Her dark eyebrows furrowed, creasing together in the way that he had grown so fondly of in their six short nights together. Then, unstoppably so, the train pulled away from the station, the whistle ripping through the calm blue sky. He looked back to see her dark, braided hair gracefully retreating down the platform.

In the diner in New York, he thumbed the rim of the white porcelain cup. The red liquid breathed ghostly vapor up into his face, obscuring the vision that at this time, his dim eyes did not possess. He only saw Santa Fe.

He remembered the first time their eyes met, through the dimly lit cigarette smoke hanging heavy on the wood-paneled walls of that bar of which the name now escaped him. He recalled the poor excuse for a joke he said to her, and how she laughed that beautiful laugh that could paint the night stars in the sky and make the birds sit and listen on any given morning.

When the bar closed down, they walked home, arm in arm, like they had known each other their whole lives. And what a beautiful life it would have been—and in that moment, it was. They talked like they had only known each other and no other thing. The night had been warm, he remembered well, the light breeze playfully coaxed them home.

The shack was a dismal thing, but with her there it seemed more than enough. He was staying there to finish writing the book that he had promised his publisher back in the city, he told her. There was simply no money to go around, but when he'd come back, he'd have her stay with him at the nicest hotel and eat at the best restaurants in town. She laughed and smiled and rubbed her fingers through his hair.

"Anything else you'd like?"

"What?" He said, his vision returning to fluorescent light of the diner—returning back to New York and the life that seemed so painfully in front of him now.

"I said, do you want anything else? You've been working on that cup of tea for a while now," said the waitress, as she furrowed her dark brows and crossed her arms.

"No, I'm good. Thank you."

"Sounds good, I'll just leave this here," she placed the check at the edge of the table and turned and left him with his deep sunset colored tea. The steam had ceased, and he watched the stained-glass smoothness of the red liquid inside the white cup.

He sipped it and felt it flow down his throat. Sweet and dark and longing. Then he put on his coat, put a few dollars on the table and walked out into the brisk city air. The western sun blazed through the windows.

I Finally Get a Morning with You

Cathy Socarras Ferrell

laze in bed
no startle of alarm
unclench my jaw
no begrudging kickstart rush
into another day
just a warm rollover
the crook of your neck
your breath is sour
my mouth tastes stale
I kiss you anyway
your hands begin to wake
you never call me baby or sweetheart
take my hand
press my scars and songs to your lips
I'll take that as an endearment
you never call me baby or sweetheart
I've gotten more morning-breath-scented I love yous than I can count
you never leave without looking me in the eye
I'll take that too

Slaked

Patricia Farrell

I am unending thirst
a wandering shadow

prey to both lush memories
& regrets for streams gone dry

until the sight of an apple tree
pulls me forward

& the thought
of piercing crisp flesh

of crushing it to my mouth
fills me with such longing

& when I am finally sated
a sweet scent coils up

of late summer yellow fruit
in our now dead orchard

& such abundance
we consumed

crushed underfoot
& the smell

of your soft breath

    apple juice on my lips

        pulp on your tongue

Shadowland

Daniel Edward Moore

Summer's shame for melting
                    the body's chilling belief in God
is sometimes enough to forgive the sky
                    for exotic dreams that wax and wane
as branches do a sign of the cross
                    above a pile of burning leaves.

We did everything right until we couldn't,
                    and so asked wrong to be our friend.
But mortality refused to lose its way
                    in the shadowland where men like me
beat each other's hearts with light—
                    those gorgeous fists of untamed love
doing what they do best.

Angles of Memory

Geo. Staley

As I walked the beach this morning
and neared the rock I'd taken a favorite photo
of my wife, now gone,
I blinked.

The photos of the now empty rock
I'd shared for 6 years to capture my loss
weren't of *the* rock
but one 30 paces closer to the ocean.
Was this caused by the slant of the morning sun?
The yearly fall accumulation of sand?
Sadness fogging my thoughts?

This blip in my usually good memory
reminded me that for 25 yrs. I'd told my students
my wretched handwriting was attributable
to a comment on my 3rd grade report card:
　　　His handwriting is like chicken scrawl.
Until I found the report card
　　　with no such comment.

Then I think of the grandmother who,
        moments before the car accident,
realized the plantation she vividly recalled
visiting as a child
(and had insisted it was on *this* rural Georgia road)
was in another state.

My slight lapses in memory
have caused no harm,
certainly no crashes
that led to the likes of The Misfit .
Yet.

My Body Is a Pool Hall
—*after Larry Levis*

Eric W. Schramm

Whose walls mellow with cigarette smoke
to a Viennese, imperial yellow. My breath—
all those rings—clouds the way out, so, yes,
why not stay another round

                              —whose slate green
skins blush with billowed stain clouds
from sticks, swung pell-mell, knocking
over bottles gushing their adulation
across the felt. All breathless is the moment
when you slide the cue through
that strange bridge of fingers and visualize
a thimble full of perfection

                              —whose bar
is mahogany-hewn, shaped by the hands
of German immigrants come to St. Louis
to work the brewery, the mill, the river.
They wanted a Thursday-to-Saturday shrine—
a broad back to hold them up, a home for elbows—
that they owned from start to finish.

Something to sand and lathe; to rest a paycheck on
and a mug, leaving circles of sweat
laid over and again with each sip;
to lean steady on as they, with a careful breath,
whisper to the small of the neck of Elisabeth,
Mary, or Magda perched on the next stool,
hoping for *Yes, let's go,*
door keys clattering with glee

      —whose jukebox
voice wails late into the night of endless love,
dumps, and long-draught drawn-out blues.
That's the juke's way, played by the room,
given to a drunk's whim with clumsy fingers—
F-9, not the desired F-4. Oh, careless tune,
indifferent needle. Lord, love that round
-and-round kiss

      —whose neighbor
fixed up the building next door. That storefront
once held a church that took the dying
line from the jukebox and made good on it
Sunday morning. Most of the hungover folks
didn't know exactly which dark, musty interior
was which, except for the tie cinched around the neck,
tight grip of sheer hose, and ill-fit shiny black shoes
made godliness known by the soul wedged
into a too small box. The church is now
"Harmony Furnishings," a fixture store

of designer knobs, switch plates, and deadbolts.
All glittery new in the sun.

        —whose bones
are old beams, weak limbs, plaster
with varicose veins, bulbs slow
to illumination, and other lower ways to live.
My super-structure sags lonely
in the new sunlight breaking across
the neighborhood with rehabs, gym memberships,
and double strollers

        —whose intervention
by concerned family is planned for after closing
when all of my dependents have wandered home,
and I am alone in the circle of light shone
bright by their best intentions: *we're worried*
with how you treat your body—
They want me to upgrade, to re-imagine
my use. To strip my past for a longer, healthier,
happier future in their image

        —whose customers
come closer to noon with each successive week,
with each turn of the lock in the great doors of the factories,
where they touched the machines in their command,
reveling in the thrum of a process running smoothly,
thoughtless, perfect. What's unclear is whether
we are here for a siege or a wake

My Body Is a Pool Hall

　　　　　　　　　　　　　—whose pulse is the rise
and fall of voices: the man turning a glass in his hands,
whispering his order; the woman thanking her friends
for "being there" as she wipes the white veil
from her face to down another shot;
and the pool balls with their constant
punctuation. Stand still on Saturday night
and listen to the crackle and murmur of voices,
rising and falling from one side of the room
to the next, like waves in a box, like a proof
for life. There must be voices. They animate me—all
of this tumbling inside. They pay the bills.
They keep turned on the neon signs
that shout back to the darkness
and display my simple offerings for you.

There and Back

Phil Wetjen

"It just seems to me that we're a lightning rod for this sort of thing." Bill paused and expelled a breath in an angry rush. His hands clenched the steering wheel tighter.

"I mean, look, there must have been at least thirty others involved. And yet there was nobody else down there, waiting around in the cold like we were. So obviously, they let everyone else know it was called off, but not us."

"Jesus," he added, looking out his side window, and away from her.

"There's really no use dwelling on it," Irene said in a low voice. "Let's just make the best of it and enjoy—."

"All the times this has happened to us, Christ, I just don't believe it." He glanced in her direction to gauge her reaction, but she was watching the road ahead, her face expressionless.

"And the damndest thing is," he went on, "I'm sure it wasn't intentional. Oh, God, it never is. No one has it out for us or anything. Pure random chance. We just—we just attract this sort of thing."

"Something in our past lives, I suppose," she said with a sniff.

He looked at her suspiciously. She knew better than to make light of his interest in Eastern religions. If she intended to stop his diatribe, this was the wrong point to start from. But she was smiling, still looking down the road.

He smiled too, loosening up a bit. "But you'll admit I've got a point, right?"

She looked at him, still smiling. "Of course you've got a point. But get your eyes on the road and let's forget it and enjoy this scenery."

"Yeah, yeah," he laughed. "The same scenery we saw a few hours ago going the other way." The anger had left his voice. Maybe now they could rationally look at this seemingly powerful ability of theirs to attract hassles, as he called them. And maybe even laugh at it.

"Like in a restaurant, or a line at the theatre, or a stand or booth or anything. God, it's like we're invisible," he said. "Remember at the fair?"

She burst out laughing. "I felt so sorry for you."

"Yeah, yeah," he said. "And how many other times. God only know the countless, infinite, astounding, sickening number of other times it's happened."

"You've got to assert yourself more, that's all," she broke in, interrupting his oration.

"That's not all," he snapped, but then calmed down enough to add, "but you're right, it sure wouldn't hurt me. You really are better in crowds and stuff."

"Don't worry buddy," she laughed. "I'll fight to the front from now on for your hotdogs."

"Alright, alright," he said, grinning.

They stopped talking for a moment, watching the alternating forests and fields they were passing. Rarely, one of the fields had a house on it, but on the whole they were empty.

"Sometimes it really galls me, though," he said. He just couldn't drop the topic. "And what caps it, the crowning blow, is that whenever we don't want service, or attention, don't want to be seen —God, it's like we're on a stage, or in a spotlight in a prison compound. I tell you, we're just meek or something. We just can't avoid this sort of thing."

Saying that got most of his feelings out. They drove on in a companionable silence, seeming to enjoy that same scenery they had passed that morning. Though it was still a misty day, things had opened up since their first time through, and they were able to see a lot more detail along the road. Besides that, he had always maintained that driving the same road in a different direction was, on the whole, a new experience.

"Damn." He spat out the word suddenly. He let up completely on the gas and the car slowed.

"What is it?" She said, alarmed. She looked all around.

"Damn, damn, damn." He snapped out the words intently, but not loudly. He put on a blinker and was braking and edging toward the shoulder.

"Is something wrong with the car?" she said.

"No," he said, too busy with handling the car to add more explanation. Two wheels, then four went onto the dirt, and cars began to pass by them on their left.

"I just saw a cat laying on the other side of the road. I think it's been hit."

"Where?" she said. She shifted away from him in the seat and looked behind them.

He looked in the mirror. "You can't see. Too far back."

They had been stopped for a moment now. He drew in a breath and pushed it out deliberately, a hard sigh. His hands were still on the wheel, and he looked straight ahead.

"Maybe it's just lying there, not hurt at all," she said.

"Maybe," he said. "But I doubt it. Not on a cold day like today."

They sat still a moment. She waited for him to make a move.

"Damn," he said, softly this time. "I'm sure it's hurt. We've got to go back."

"It's definitely alive then?"

He nodded, and sat up straight in the seat as she turned to face forward again.

"There's a place to turn around," he said, pointing ahead to a small side road. They drove slowly along the bumpy shoulder toward it. When they reached it, they had to wait for cars to pass by before they could turn around. There were at least half a dozen from each direction. They found themselves watching the faces of the people in the cars that passed. Some faces were intent on the road. Some were looking at them, either curiously, or idly. A few were looking back behind them.

When the road was empty they pulled out. He went through two gear changes and about a quarter-mile without seeing anything on the road. Maybe, hopefully, the cat had gotten off the road on its own. Maybe it hadn't been hurt at all.

They topped a slight rise, and he saw it.

"There it is."

He again went through the ritual of signaling, braking, and edging off the pavement. The cat was just off the road, on the shoulder. Its body was twisted in an odd way. The rear legs and hindquarters seemed to be ninety degrees off from the rest of the body. It wasn't an extreme twist. It was a position similar to ones in which cats contort themselves while cleaning or stretching in the sun.

The cat looked in their direction as the car approached, but didn't move away. Bill stopped the car quite close to the cat, with two wheels still on the pavement, to cover the cat, to protect it from the cars on the road.

A few cars had bunched up behind them as they went off the road, and these were going by, now that they were out of the way.

"Let me look," he said, not looking at her. He glanced in the outside mirror and stepped out. As he walked to the front of the car and looked down, he didn't see the cat.

He looked up at her. "Ha, he's gone."

He walked a few steps more before he saw the cat. He stepped over to it, and squatted down.

"Easy buddy," he said, very softly. He put one hand on the ground and leaned over the animal. The cat had somehow rolled, or pulled itself from its former position to a place closer to the ditch, away from the road. It must have been afraid of their car.

The effort of moving the width of the car had taken its toll. The cat was breathing hard, almost gasping. Its tongue was out and had blood on it. Its eyes were glassy, the pupils large. But Bill knew the cat saw him. Its eyes had shifted toward him, despite their distant focus.

"OK, buddy," he said.

Bill didn't know what to do. He stood up, and glanced at Irene. Their eyes met. Hers were questioning. He came around to her door.

"He's hurt bad," he said. "At least I think he is". Bill looked down at her. "It's hard to tell, though. Remember Jane's dog that got hit on Easter?"

"Keeks," she said.

"Yeah, Keeks. Keeks looked about dead when I carried him to the station wagon. But a few days at the vet and he was fine."

He looked towards the cat, then back at her.

"Well, I'm going to get him off the road. I'll put him on the grass over there, and then maybe look around for some people. There's at least one house over there." He pointed off to the right as he strode back to the cat.

As he squatted down again, he thought that the cat looked a little better. Its head was resting on the ground, and it seemed to be breathing a little easier. The head rose as he leaned near. The cat looked his way for a moment, then rested its head again. It seemed to be less alarmed by his appearance than the first time.

Bill slid one hand under the cat's front shoulder, and one under the hindquarters. He spread his fingers wide and supported some of the weight with his wrist too, hoping to cushion his load.

"Here we go now, buddy. You just take it easy." Bill spoke in a low voice, melodically, as if reassuring a child. As he spoke he pivoted on his heels, stood, and walked carefully off the shoulder and up a small bank of grass. He glanced around for a spot to place the cat and saw a piece of cardboard. It was wet, though.

Turning his head away from the cat, he called in a low voice to Irene. "Hey, do we have anything I can put him on? It's all wet over here."

She looked back doubtfully, but turned to the back seat. Meanwhile, Bill put the cat down on the cardboard, and jogged over to the car. As he reached it Irene turned to him.

"How's this?" It was a piece of black plastic.

"Perfect," he said.

"It's what I use to cover the windshield on frosty mornings."

He took it and returned to the cat. Laying the plastic next to the cardboard, he kneeled down and was able to slide the cat to the plastic with a minimum of lifting, and he hoped, a minimum of pain. Then he stood for a moment and looked to the houses, which were a bit further down the road, and about one hundred yards in.

"I'm going to check those houses and see if anyone knows this cat," he called. He paused and looked around, from her to the houses. Then he looked up and down the road, searching for other houses. There were none visible.

"Why don't you pull off the road better," he said. "You could even pull into that road." He indicated a dirt sideroad, or perhaps it was just a driveway, that seemed to lead to the houses he saw. "I'll cut across the field here."

He took a step on the way, but stopped, bent over, and put the piece of cardboard over the lower half of the cat. He gazed at it briefly, then started out across the field.

Before he was halfway across, Bill began to think he should have gone the long way, along the road, to the driveway. The grass was sparse in the field, and the rain the past week had made it muddy. His shoes were getting heavy with the mud. After a few more steps, things seemed to improve, so he kept on his course. He guessed that his shoes had collected the maximum amount of mud they could carry, so things couldn't get any worse. His attention left his feet and focused on the houses.

He couldn't tell if there were one or two homes. There was actually a complex of buildings that seemed part of a farm. There was one building occupied, a large barn, a smaller barn that was being used as a garage, and another building, with glass windows, that could also be occupied.

He began thinking that if these people, if they were home, didn't know about the cat, then they would be stuck with it.

Just then he saw a man appear from behind a small truck and begin walking toward the smaller house. Bill walked faster through the mud, hoping to arrive near the house before the man could disappear. Walking faster kicked up mud on his pantlegs, and he felt water seeping into his socks. Ignoring this, he kept up his pace and as he came into what he considered the yard of the house, he was relieved to see the man standing there. Maybe he had caught a glimpse of Bill crossing the field, and was waiting for him.

Bill decided that his best bet would be to get an explanation out as quickly as possible, before anyone could question his being there.

"Hi, I was just driving down the highway, towards Bainbridge, and I saw a cat lying in the road, on the other side." Bill wondered if he had made it clear he hadn't hit the animal. "I got him off the road. He's on the bank over there." Bill gestured with his hand in that direction without turning his face away from the man. "I was wondering if anyone around here owns the cat. Or knows about it. It's a gray one," he added.

Aside from nodding when he first appeared, the man had made no sign, either positive or negative, that he knew the cat.

"I can't help you," he said. "You'll have to ask these people." He nodded towards the house.

"Oh, you don't live here," Bill said.

"No," he said.

No explanation of why he was there followed this, and Bill was beginning to wonder what to ask next when the man added, "She'll be out in a minute".

Bill acknowledged this with a light hand motion, relieved that he wouldn't have to go knocking on doors to find someone.

Just then a woman appeared at a door. She only stayed there long enough to let out a small black dog, after which she disappeared into the house. In the brief moment she was visible, Bill saw only that she was a large woman, wore glasses, and didn't seem very easy going, by the way she had jerked the door open and shut.

The dog made its way toward Bill and the man, barking, but not in a vicious manner. It was more of a testing bark, to see if the intruders would run. When it reached them, it jumped up on Bill, putting its front paws on his thigh. Bill leaned down and petted it, rubbing it around its ears, which always pleased the dog his family had when he was a child. He wondered if the dog could smell the cat on him, and more, if it could sense that the cat was hurt. The dog didn't give any indication of sensing anything other than Bill.

A few long moments went by. Bill occupied himself by continuing to stroke the dog. He avoided looking at the man.

A sudden noise of clashing metal shifted their collective attention to the far end of the house. The same woman pushed her way past a wooden and tin door that looked like it had been through many years of repair. She held a yellow slip of paper in her hand, and picked her way through the wet lawn towards them. When she got to them she handed the slip to the man.

"There you go. That should settle us till later," she said.

"Sure will," he replied.

During this interchange Bill reflected that the woman was not as large as he first thought, and that she did not act unfriendly.

The man turned and began walking off to the truck. The woman turned to Bill.

"Hello," she said. It was more of a question than a greeting, as if she had said "Yes?"

"Hi," said Bill. "I was just driving toward Bainbridge and I saw a cat lying on the other side of the road. It's been hit. I got it off the road. It's alive, but it's hurt. I'm just trying to find out if anyone here knows it."

As he said all this, Bill was musing on how close it was to his speech to the man. He found he couldn't even remember how he had phrased it the first time.

"Well," she said, "we've got a few cats around here." She glanced all around. Bill looked around too, but didn't see any cats.

"This is a gray one," he said. "With short hair."

"Is it a tiger?" she asked.

Bill wasn't really sure what to say to this. He knew it wasn't a solid gray cat, but he couldn't remember what pattern its fur had. The only cats called tigers he remembered had more of an orange coloring.

"It's sort of a tiger, I guess," he said. She didn't reply. "It's right over on the bank there." He turned his head and pointed.

"Well, I guess I'll have to take a look," she said, with some reluctance. It seemed to Bill to be more reluctance over leaving the house than having to look at the cat, but he couldn't say why. "Just let me put the dog in."

She did this quickly, and the two of them started across the field.

"You wore the wrong footgear for this," she said, as they neared the halfway point. Bill looked at her and saw her looking at his shoes. Rather than making him feel sheepish, as a remark like this normally would, Bill felt that somehow the woman appreciated his slogging through the mud for this cat. He glanced at her footgear, and saw that she had on a pair of ankle-high plastic boots. While looking at her feet, he remembered Irene and looked down to the driveway, but couldn't see the car. The bank the cat was on increased in height down there, and he decided the car must be in a hollow behind it.

They were close to the cat now. As they approached it, Bill saw that the cardboard had fallen off the animal's lower body. He and the woman walked to within a yard of the cat and stopped, both looking down.

Besides throwing off the covering cardboard, the cat had rolled over onto its other side. Its upper body and head were rocking back and forth, and its breathing was in sharp gasps. Its mouth was wide open, and the blood on its tongue was now bright red. The cat was obviously in great pain, and Bill felt a surge of fear and guilt. Perhaps he had hurt it more by moving it. Could he have done as much damage as the car had done, by carrying the cat wrong?

"Oh, I'm sorry, Tigger." the woman said. She said it to the cat.

"He's yours, then," Bill said.

"Yes. We've had him for years." She paused, thinking of the years.

Bill's feelings were filled with the cat's pain, but under that he felt a sense of relief that the cat was no longer his responsibility.

"I don't know if there's anything we can do." she said.

"Could a vet help him?" Bill asked. "I don't know anything about these things. Maybe it's not that bad."

"No, I think it's bad," she said.

"Can I carry him back for you anyway?" he asked.

"Yes, I guess so," she said. She thought for a moment. "The barn would be OK." She pointed to a small barn, behind her house, that Bill hadn't even noticed during his look around.

Just then Bill heard footsteps behind him. A man was approaching along the bank. He looked at them and the cat and seemed to immediately understand the situation.

"Tigger's been hit, Dale," the woman said. The man nodded slowly.

Bill said, "Does it look bad to you? I don't know much about these things. Could a vet help him?"

"No, he's dying," the man said. He said it flatly, not with disinterest, but with acceptance, a note of compassion, and with finality. "Nothing to be done," he said quietly. After a moment, he walked by them and went towards the house. Bill watched him go off. He saw the woman watching him too. Their eyes returned to the cat at the same moment.

"Can I still carry him in for you?" he said.

"Yes, go ahead."

Bill knelt and slid his hands under the plastic to lift the cat. As he did, the cat cried out. It was a sound so far from a meow that Bill could hardly believe the cat had made it. It was a bit like the sounds he had heard of cats in heat, or cats working up to a fight, but much more intense than either of those. He drew his hands back quickly. He was surprised to see that the fingers of his right hand had blood on them. The cat must have been cut on its side facing the ground, although he hadn't noticed it before. He stood up.

"I'd better not," he said.

The cat was twisting in agony. Its head jerked spasmodically once or twice. Then its head and eyes turned straight up, into the air, and suddenly, the life went out of the eyes, and the head began sinking slowly back to the ground.

"That's it," Bill said. He knew the cat was dead. He had never seen anything die before, and was surprised that the moment was so unmistakable. The eyes were now lifeless, but it would have been hard to say in what way they were different than a few moments before.

Bill knelt back down and pulled the cardboard over the cat, and stood up.

"I'm sorry," he said.

"Oh. It's not your fault," the woman said. "You were good to stop."

"Yeah," Bill said softly. "Well, I guess I'll head out now."

"OK," she said. "Thanks for helping".

"Goodbye."

"Goodbye."

Bill turned and strode off along the bank towards the driveway. When he caught sight of the car, he was surprised to see Irene in the driver's seat. It took him a moment to remember that she had to drive the car off the road and into the driveway. It seemed a long time since he had left her.

He felt like driving. He needed something real to focus on right now. Despite this, he went around to the passenger side. Explaining why he needed to drive would be too much right now, too much like explaining the cat. It was too soon for any explaining.

"Let's go," he said, once he was inside. He didn't look at her.

Irene could see his turmoil. She started the car up and did a tight turn to get back on the highway. Bill was grateful for her prompt action. He knew she must be wondering what had happened. On the road, he might get a grip on all this.

Once on the highway, Irene drove in silence for a few miles. She didn't talk until she saw Bill's clenched fists open, and he began rubbing one hand with the other.

"Did you find the owners?" she asked.

The question forced Bill away from the image of the cat at its moment of death. He couldn't stop seeing its eyes.

"Yes," he said. "They weren't very upset. I mean they were sad, but quietly. There was no carrying on or anything." He paused, looking out the windshield. "Lots less upset than me, in fact." He smiled sadly, looking back to her. She turned from the road to him. He saw her question.

"He died. He was in agony. I've never seen anything die before."

The time they had spent riding, rather than widening the distance from the event, seemed to narrow it. The full impact of the death was beginning to overtake Bill. Sadness and fatigue were overwhelming him.

"It was good he died. He was in agony. He was crying out, like a person. He couldn't move and he couldn't lay still, and he just cried. And then it was over, and his whole body relaxed, and he stopped crying."

Bill was crying now, and Irene was too. She bit her lower lip and focused her eyes on the road and put her right hand out to him. His eyes were crying steadily now. His feelings had held back until that moment.

A few miles passed. He gradually came out of his feelings enough to be calm and talk more.

"Well," he said, "if Tigger was one of your Roman Catholics, then I guess we'll see him in heaven." He dried his eyes with his knuckles. "And if he's a Buddhist, he'll owe us one next time around. Right, buddy?" The tears came again.

"You were good to stop, you know," she said. "I know you didn't want to."

"Yeah, well somebody had to," he said.

"Yes, somebody did."

"Like I told you before, it's always us."

"That's OK."

"Yes, it is."

Epistemological Concerns Around the Best Poem Ever

Patrick S. Rogers

—*for Steve Albini*

On our way to the timeclock, all my co-workers,
these warehouseman slap skin, fist pump,
say this is the best poem ever. Everyone else says
they like the ones that admit a body's vulnerability,
and not popping Achilles or cut-off fingers
or eleven hundred pound steel reels smashing heads,
pulverizing vertebrae. No, the one's that know
a body's limit; a slipping grip, vein coming to the surface,
beads of sweat, the musk of labor.
Pedro asks *what's epistemology*, and I say
how the fuck should I know. *Well, this is your poem,
you're supposed to know what words mean.*
Look, I just want to get back to the place with the fist pumps,
the fist bumps, the sly high five, the laughter at the time clock
where they say this is the best poem ever.
They all trump up the stairs and the din of their laughter fades
as I flick off the warehouse lights and I feel my way to the door,
tripping over something and landing on hands and knees;
slick with wet I sniff for blood, oil, gasoline on the ground in the dark

And it is then I remember some guy much smarter than me saying
ritual is what makes time habitable
and then Pedro, the first one down
dressed in his home clothes *what'dya know?*
Look who needs a hand! Then says as he helps me up
I hope this makes it in the poem.
Pedro, I'm fairly certain this is what
makes this the best poem ever. He puts up his hand,
spreads his five fingers wide and says *Bien* as we slap hi-five.

Like All Good Rain

Sam Spring

It starts with a rumble,
Deep and low out over the
Horizon. Rolling over the
Springtime plains with their
Grasses so vibrant—so
Very, very green. Finally, the
Fall. It showers the wetrock,
Darkening the ground,
Blurring the landscape.
And when it reaches
The sea, well, I'm sure
It must disappear, like all
Good rain does, into the
Vastness of that opposite
Horizon.

Gonesong

Colleen S. Harris

It's the gone things that stay
to haunt you, tickling
your nose, brushing your cheek
when you thought them far
and forgotten. They pop out
in unlikely spaces, spear
your breath at a half-recognized face.
Some think death is the worst
but it's the living that gets you,
the small things, fresh laundry,
a woodsy cologne whose name
you've forgotten,
the gold earring you lose
that ruins the pair. The void
gets smaller with time, but
more dense, when it hits you
it bowls you over, yanks you back
in time to remember every word,
the rattle-hum of the gearshift
on that blue hatchback Pontiac,
the green spark of his eyes
when he put his foot through

the television when his team lost.
The tune you crave others
hear with horror:

               the sound of a fist
striking deep gouges in drywall,
a beloved voice raining
curses like fire from the sky.
This silence that's left is cold,
and with no one but God listening,
you cry into your pillow
whispering *come home.*

Psalm of Heavy Persuasion

Daniel Edward Moore

Oh, blessed barricade, my dazzling detour,
do what you must. Teach me to stay.

Let moss, rust and the choir of corrosion
proclaim your immovable love.

Let darkness and its hungry eyes
be consoled by the concrete vision of you
not taking the light for granted.

If more is needed, I can be sure
cracks in the stone will pray like they did
for flesh to become fire.

Shock

Jonathan Wlodarski

Before Dmitry woke up, Natasha was checking the forecast for at least an hour. An inescapable storm, bright red on the radar, was chugging toward them. Anticipation—or was it her allergy?—prickled the skin on her scalp. When he finally got up, Dmitry leaned in for a kiss, inhaled. "Storm coming," he said. He swore he could smell the change on her skin, that she exuded a lightning scent.

"Stop pretending I smell different," Natasha said. She'd never noticed this smell he talked about.

"But you do. A wet, coppery base with notes of ozone and... hmm...sweet alyssum, maybe? Definitely a floral, but I can't place it—yet," he said. He worked for a perfume company, designing new fragrances. "What's the forecast like?" He rose from the bed, adjusted his glasses; the lenses were thick like glass cinder blocks, his vision without them mere smears of color. His eyesight kept getting worse, and he joked his sense of smell compensated for his vision. "You can't imagine how *awake* I feel, smelling everything so keenly," he said.

She checked one of the dozen weather apps on her phone again. "Storms should hit here in about an hour," she said.

"I'm gonna shower. Have you already called off?" said Dmitry from the bathroom.

She didn't answer, raising her arm to her nose to sniff: as always, nothing. If only she could detect this lightning scent. Maybe just a whiff would quiet the ache in her head. It was the lightning that Natasha had to avoid, because it made her skin burn and her throat swell shut in anaphylactic shock. It was the lightning Natasha felt crackling in the air, that started to deaden her nerve endings from miles away. And it was the lightning that Natasha couldn't resist, but no one seemed to understand that.

"Why would you go outside during a thunderstorm? You know it makes you sick!" her father had shouted as he stabbed her with epinephrine when she was nine—two doses, since one wasn't strong enough to clear up the hives and open her airway.

Natasha couldn't explain. Even just sitting indoors during a passing storm made her go numb gradually as her allergy came on. But it didn't matter that it could kill her—all she wanted was to jump-start her circuitry with the crackle of airborne electricity. Sometimes, lightning would strike so close she swore she could feel the photons and alpha particles surging through the glass of the bedroom window, tingling across her skin even as it went numb. Why wouldn't she want to feel that on a large scale, that jolt to bring her back to life like a frog in science class?

Dmitry came out of the bathroom, glasses fogged. He wore a pair of obnoxious boxers, plum purple with bright red arrows that overlapped, a clamorous frenzy rushing to point to his crotch.

"I thought we agreed to get rid of those," she said. "They're hideous."

"Only if you get rid of that bra I can never unhook. That was the deal," he said. Natasha picked up a bra from the floor—the un-hookable one—and threw it at him. He tried to dodge it, but it landed on his shoulder. His depth perception was iffy. He pulled it off his shoulder and fiddled with the clasps. "Shit, I snapped it." He showed her how the prongs of the clasp were bent the wrong way, ripping away from the fabric. He shrugged and tossed it on the floor. "Did you hear about that kid with platinum teeth on the news last night? I couldn't tell if you were asleep when it was on," he said.

Natasha kept her face neutral as she checked the weather maps again.

"The dentist pulled all his teeth and he bled to death. Do you think he was a patient of Anita's?"

Hearing her sister's name tensed her muscles. "I don't know. He might have been. She's so popular these days. How am I supposed to keep track?" One of the apps' forecasts said it was supposed to snow, an absurd prediction.

"Have you talked to her lately?" said Dmitry.

"She's been at this for, what, fifteen years?" Natasha said. "I don't need to baby her."

"Okay. I'll call her later, I guess," he said. "Did you talk to your boss?"

Natasha closed the weather apps and texted her supervisor. He replied within twenty seconds—he knew to check for Natasha's texts on rainy mornings. *Just review the bug report and processor presentations by end of day.* He grumbled every time she called off—she knew he thought she was making it up, but she told him to imagine that she had a sensitive heart condition instead. That seemed to calm him down.

Thunder broke as Dmitry knotted his tie. "You sure you'll be okay? I can call off if you need," he said.

"Don't," she said. She looked up from her phone and adjusted his tie again. He'd left it slightly askew.

"If something happens, Tash, I'll be upset with myself," he said. "They told me I need to use some of my vacation days anyway. Last

time it stormed, I was home, and the time before, the storm only last-
ed forty-five minutes. But today my phone says rain for at least three
hours."

"I'll be fine. I survived thunderstorms before I met you," Nata-
sha said. She smiled, though she resented how diminished his faith in
her was. She was in her thirties—she could handle herself.

"Okay. I'll check in later," he said. "Wish me luck: today's the
big meeting for the final version of my *mystery client's* new perfume."
Mystery client meant celebrity, probably a reality TV star who wanted
to slap their name on a bottle of something Dmitry made. He had to
sign a nondisclosure agreement every time he worked with famous
people.

Once Natasha was alone, she wrapped herself in blankets and
stared out the giant window that was the west wall of their bedroom.
After their third date, when Dmitry invited her to his apartment, she'd
refused to enter. "I'll feel like a fish in an aquarium. Drop some flakes
in, *glub glub*," she'd said. She hadn't told him that seeing the giant pane
of glass reminded her of the one-way mirror they'd used to observe her
at the hospital when she was a child. But she got used to the window,
and when she moved in eighteen months later, Dmitry had offered to
let his lease lapse, to move to a basement apartment, but she refused.
"The view is too nice," she'd said.

Really, she liked the window because it let her watch the light-
ning.

Natasha's phone buzzed: Dmitry. *I'm at wirk. Still ok? Hssn't
started rainong hrre yet.* His texts were often riddled with typos, small
ones autocorrect had decided to assimilate; she wasn't sure if they were
because of how bad his eyes were or because he was too focused on
other things to hammer out each letter correctly.

A few droplets here. Feeling ok, she sent back. Not long after, the rain picked up, droplets becoming insistent sheets of water, and she could see the heavier clouds looming. She opened her laptop and scrolled through the presentation she was missing. They'd vote on the processor chip manufacturing contract the next day and she wanted to know what she was voting for.

Brian, thanks for sending this along. She was mid-email when she first heard the thunder, a rumble that seemed to vibrate through the building's foundations. She finished her email quickly and turned on the weather. TV weather was comforting: all that soothing elevator music and genial meteorologists pointing to storm cells on their maps.

Her phone buzzed again. *Srartimg to pixk up here. You gpod stiol?*

Yes. Get back to work. I'm fine. She turned her attention to the television.

"Looks like we're gonna be in this storm for quite a while, everyone," said Steve MacLear, the dashing weatherman. Of the local broadcasters, he was Natasha's least favorite. The internet said he didn't have a degree in meteorology, having allegedly been hired by the network for his good looks alone. How could she trust his reportage?

She pulled the blankets above her head. More thunder, louder and closer. Then, visible even from beneath the fabric and behind her eyelids—lightning. She peeked her head out from the covers, just in time to see white-hot forks zigzagging in all directions, sparkling in the windowpanes and burning in her retinas. It was a few miles off, but already her fingertips had started to go numb.

She opened the gardening simulator app she was testing. The startup she worked for made mobile games, and she was stuck as lead QA tester. She should have been CTO, but her boss was probably wary to promote someone who stayed home so often. It didn't matter—she liked testing the apps. She loved this game's mundane tasks, watering flowers and pruning dead leaves; she'd leveled her beds to "community garden" status. The lead developer told her she was still twenty-five hours of playtime from maxing out at "botanical garden."

Her favorite feature was the game's location-based integration of weather information: real-life conditions were mirrored in the simulated garden, so when it stormed, she could be inside the rain without ever looking up from the palm of her hand. She was trying to dig tiny drain ditches—she had just gotten her lilies to bloom and didn't want to rip them out—but her lifeless fingertips were challenging her precision and she kept routing the water into her violets.

The screen flashed and a notification popped up: "Oh no! Your garden was struck by lightning! Some of your flowers got destroyed!" She set the phone down, surprised. Never before had lightning actually struck in the game. The thrill, the temptation, loomed even in her pretend garden. Thunder rattled the windows. Sometimes, the shaking was so loud that Natasha and Dmitry were convinced the glass would shatter and their bedroom would flood, but the building superintendent assured them the glass was break-resistant.

Natasha's numbness spread up her hands and arms. She stared into the storm clouds, deep purple contusions chugging along. Her phone lit up. There had been a few buzzes as she played, but she'd ignored them. Probably all Dmitry, panicking that she as ignoring him. But the messages were from an unsaved number, one whose sequence she had memorized long ago: Anita's. *Just checking in. Are you okay?* Her sister sent another message, a picture of a potted pink African violet next to the vase of orange tiger lilies. *My new office decorations. Just like mom's garden.* Natasha's heart thudded.

She threw her phone onto the ground. The screen shattered. The picture of the flowers, spider-webbed from the cracks in the glass, taunted her from below. She sank back into the pillows, shielding her face with the blanket. She counted as she breathed—a good distraction she'd learned all the way back in kindergarten—and got into the six hundreds before her phone buzzed. Dmitry again.

Storm us prettu close now. You still ik? What's westhrr saying?

Natasha turned the television on again. "Our radar is showing us trapped in this storm cell for at least another four hours. I'm predicting *major* flooding for some viewers!" said Steve.

Bad forecast. I'm okay, she texted, fingers gingerly pressing the broken glass. She dragged herself to the living room to grab bug reports from work. So much paperwork for her to wade through. Sometimes, when she landed in the hospital with one of her allergic reactions, she had coworkers bring paperwork to her so she could review it while the swelling in her throat went down. She stayed on the floor, trying to organize the papers, her fingers fumbling, the numbness turning them uncooperative.

The first time Natasha had gone numb was terrifying. A storm had rolled in while she'd slept, thunder booming so loud it woke her. When she sat up, she couldn't feel her torso bend, couldn't tell if her lips and tongue were moving as she tried to call for her father. All she could manage was shapeless yelling that brought him running. But now she was used to it, performing a series of dexterity exercises: flexing her fingers, rubbing the tips against the palms of her hands, trying to acquaint the dead skin to itself. She practiced touching her thumbs to the rest of her fingers one by one.

Her phone vibrated again, an angry hornet sound against the hardwood. Longer this time: a call, the string of numbers—two threes, six-seven-eight in sequence—flashing. Natasha froze. Anita. She leered at the phone, willing it silent. The screen darkened; she relaxed, but it glowed to life again. This was Anita's game. She would call again and again until Natasha picked up. It had been a few months since Anita had reached out, and Natasha had hoped it meant she'd given up. She let the phone ring three times, four. Sure, she could turn off her phone, but if it was Dmitry and she didn't answer, he'd think something was wrong. Natasha was *fine*.

But if she didn't take her sister's call, then Anita would reach out to Dmitry—Dmitry, who talked to his girlfriend's older sister once a week just to check in and comfort her, something Natasha herself couldn't do anymore.

The numbness had trickled upward to her shoulders, rising to her neck and sinking into her chest. She knew she should use the bathroom soon, before the numbness traveled below her waist. More than once she had been humiliated when thunderstorms rolled through and she hadn't excused herself in time. As she walked to the bathroom, she bumped into the doorframe, still reading, trying not to look at the window as she passed by.

She was too absorbed in the paperwork to notice the broken, unhookable bra on the floor. When she stepped on it, the satin under her foot slid across the wood floor. Papers flew up as her body thudded to the ground. She grunted, then opened her eyes: her view of the window was uninterrupted. The storm was fully upon her, a maelstrom of wind, rain, lightning streaking across the sky and splitting the clouds asunder. She watched in awe, even as she felt the numbness surge down to her stomach.

During some of the worst storms, when Natasha couldn't bear to pull herself away from the window, she'd entwine herself with Dmitry, their movements an ample diversion from what happened outside their bedroom. Even then, she'd keep one eye on the window at all times, trying to use the thunder and lightning like metronomes to direct their speed and intensity. But now Dmitry wasn't there—she had nothing to call her attention away, even for a second, from the flares and fulminations just beyond her reach.

Nothing to distract her, except the persistent droning of her phone in the other room. The sound had taken root in her brain, a dull ache in her hippocampus. "Stop calling me!" she said. She reached for the bra, ripped off the broken clasp, and unbent the metal.

The electrical socket close to her sparked and smoked as she rammed the metal in. She screamed, something between a screech of pain and a shriek of ecstasy, and her skin seared back to life, her nerve endings alight like bonfires. She relished acting as a conduit for the coursing current, the electricity humming under her nails, inside her liver, around her brain.

After, she walked back to the living room, where the phone continued to rattle on the floor. Natasha bent down to retrieve it, slid her finger against the cracked glass—felt the shards slice her skin—and answered. "Hello," she said.

Anita's sigh whooshed into Natasha's ear in a staticky burst. "You're okay," she said

"Of course I am," Natasha said. She perched herself on the edge of the bed to continue watching the storm, her brain buzzing.

"Why didn't you pick up?" Anita said. "I was worried."

"I was hoping you'd forgotten about me," Natasha said. "Too busy to bother me." Her tongue felt heavy and thick in her mouth.

"I'll always make time for you," Anita said. "I care about you. I just want to help."

"I don't need your help," Natasha said. "Nobody can help me."

"That's not true!" Anita said. "Just last week I fixed a guy from New Jersey with an allergy to violin music, and last month I helped that woman that was growing rust in her ears. I could help you like I helped them." Anita, even when she was excited, never yelled.

"What about that kid with the metal teeth?" Natasha said. "Was he one of your patients?"

Silence for a moment or two. "I'm not the one who pulled his teeth," Anita said.

"But if his parents never got you involved, maybe he'd still be alive," Natasha said. "Doctors don't help!" There it was: the uptick in her voice. She couldn't keep her voice even like her sister could. The storm boomed. "I don't need you to experiment on me. It's just an allergy."

"An allergy I can cure, maybe," Anita said.

The *maybe* rang through the speaker like a funeral bell. The numbness crept into Natasha again. The shock was wearing off. The shock was setting in.

"Find someone else to experiment on," Natasha said. She inhaled, breath a little ragged. Her phone buzzed. A text from Dmitry at the top of the screen: *I have a surprise for yiu.*

"I want to make your life better," Anita said. Natasha waited for her to gasp or even hiccup, but nothing. Her sister was so composed, always. Dmitry had seen her cry once, one of the times Natasha had been hospitalized, but she'd never seen it herself. "If you'd had help when we were kids, maybe Mom wouldn't have—"

"Stop," Natasha said. She remembered how the air smelled after the lightning struck—the sharp tang of oxygen and hydrogen being rent in two—and licked her lips. She remembered how crisp everything smelled when the lightning electrified her mother; she'd run after a seven-year-old Natasha, who broke free of her stiff grasp and bee-lined for the sidewalk in front of the house. Even then, as a child, she couldn't resist the storm.

The lightning came down from the sky and crucified her moth-er—her arms flew out as she sank to the ground, into the flower beds like Dorothy into the field of poppies, but these flowers were lilies and violets, flowers they'd pick the next day to line her coffin. Natasha had been able to taste the lightning on her tongue, had felt it crackle through her hair, had sensed it supercharging her blood.

"Other people can get hurt," Anita said. "It took me *years* to get over Mom dying: I *still* can't walk past flowerboxes without looking for violets and lilies."

"I was *seven*!" Natasha said. A tear welled up in the corner of her eye, dancing and wobbling, but she blinked it away, her vision glittering iridescent with moisture. There was a sob in her throat that made her voice warble, or maybe that was just her windpipe swelling shut.

Anita cut her sister off without raising her voice. "But you're not seven now," she said. "You're still putting yourself at risk. And Dmitry—"

"Don't make him part of this," said Natasha. She watched the storm—some of the lightning was going sideways, lighting up the clouds from within.

"He's already part of it," Anita said. "D'you know what he says when we talk? The saddest things, like how he—"

"No," Natasha said, rasping. "I don't want to hear what he says." She already knew: that he woke up at night reaching for her, afraid she'd drifted outside after the weathermen had promised a storm front, that he almost left her six months ago when she tried to take a plugged-in toaster into the shower to feel the electricity. She inhaled, readying herself for a tirade, but the breath was more of a stuttering gasp. Her tongue was heavy, immobile: the socket's shock had electrified her alive, but only briefly. Now, she was numb again.

The phone vibrated against her ear again—a picture of a spherical perfume bottle, dark green, with the word "Natasha" emblazoned in copper across it. *Ta-da!*, the caption read. *Thos is the frsgrancd I've actually been wprking on. I finakly got the formula dowm.*

"Tash? That breath sounded awfully labored. You—you haven't gone outside, have you?" Anita said. Her voice was far away, tinny through the speaker when it wasn't held up to Natasha's skull.

A third buzz: *Herr's the offivual scent desxriotion: "a wet, citrus-copper base with violet and lily floral notes."* Her pulse quickened. She had never told Dmitry about her mother's flowers, but here they were again, haunting her.

"Natasha? Are you still there? Answer me." Anita's voice cracked. Natasha heard it, even from far away, like the first crack in the sidewalk before a sinkhole swallowed up the whole street. Natasha switched from Dmitry's texts back to the call. Her index finger hovered over the red "end call" circle for a moment—she pressed down, hard, hard enough to drive glass shards into her finger.

She rode the elevator down to the first floor, phone buzzing over and over. She looked down—more missed calls, plus another text from Dmitry. *Do yiu like tour surpride?* She'd answer him later. She walked into the storm, a white-hot streak of lighting racing toward her.

When My Lover Called Me Artist, I Thought of Moths

Michelle Boland

What, exactly, grows in us
with each ending—
the moth's imaginal discs, these

      organizing cells
the body will need.
Discs for eyes, for wings.

When my lover called me artist,
he built the back porch rail
upon which I hang

like a pupa.
And what stirred

      in me, amorphous mess,

added more wing
than maybe my body
      could hold. But such

strong glue,
perfect   cell division,

this defining margin
that shifts
when the body   begins

    to push itself
toward movement,

    and what I was before

mattered   only a little.

Shadows

Ty Zhang

My friends,
Your lives are lanterns strung
On the wall of shadows that is my life:
They cast the only light.
A somber picture, I know.
But wait.
Soon enough a breeze will trickle through
And the shadows will start to dance.
Between their kicking legs,
Like children or like cats,
We will play.

Key Change

Bradley Samore

Age (without which I'd never have been born)
decomposes the jazz tune I go on
writing. The staff rakes across my page: worn
brow with its five parallel wrinkles drawn
and deepening. My first teacher taught me
Every Good Boy Does Fine to memorize
the notes, and I did, but the myth, faulty,
crumbled. I clung to the rubble; watched flies
rubbing their hands, plotting my eviction;
flung myself at sages' definitions
of "good," their throats brimming with conviction;
let others pen lyrics to my questions.
      Having tried theirs and waded through regret,
      I sing my dissonance like the egret.

The Beginning of Detachment

Erik Manuel Soto

Quiet corner-coiled boy, eyes in slow drift-fall.
Forget the hour marking mother with purple badges.
Forget the sight of father fist-clenched,
drunk-faced falling on olive couch.
Crepuscular light. Imagine shadows are antlers.
Your hands, hooves, holding hibiscus.
Wipe those trailing tears.
Pretend your cheeks are covered with glittering copper.
Otherwise, dream, boy, dream.

The Rains of Amity

Eric Oman Callahan

For Emily, the road home was like driving to the dentist; fighting against a mote of dread deep in her heart even if she would never use such a dramatic word. Today however, her spirits were high, and she wasn't eyeing the fuel tank with a secret wonder of how far it could go. Even when the old station wagon coughed loudly, whined dryly and started slowing down she stayed optimistic. Stroking the felt-covered steering wheel, Emily tried to urge it forward.

"You're alright Stanley, you're alright," she cooed.

Despite her encouragement, the car wheezed like a dying horse before inevitably failing with a heavy kachunk. The power was gone and Emily had to veer into the side of the road where the loose dirt shoulder grabbed the tires and yanked the steering wheel in her hands. The tail threatened to slide away and she had to fight to keep from smashing into the low, spindly bushes that dotted the roadside. When all momentum finally stopped, she panted heavily and then screamed.

"Shit! Shit fuck shit, you shitting fuck!"

Emily slammed her hands against the dash several times and then stopped, letting out a defeated sigh. It had been more of a bad landing than a crash. Stanley had been through worse. Being honest with herself, it was a surprise that the car had lasted so long this time around. At 22 the car was two years her elder and if it could voice an opinion, it might say that the lack of regular maintenance was at fault. Stanley needed to go into the shop nearly every month, but that never happened. Instead, they just drove until it couldn't drive anymore, and then Dad would devise some mechanical bandage to keep it going a little longer, until finally they would call up Mom. She'd pay to have it fixed because: "It's the least I can do." This happened about twice a year. There were nights when Emily didn't want her help, but she seemed to be the only one. Dad never complained. They were always like that, Mom and Dad, getting along for the big stuff with easy smiles and little lies. Mom left before Emily could understand why. She was still trying to figure that one out. Most people were missing a mom or a dad it seemed though. That didn't make things better, it just made it normal.

Emily had driven to McMinnville because it had a video store. Her hometown of Amity, Oregon didn't have much besides a handful of cramped bungalows, some wineries, and a church or two. It was one of several drive-thru towns on the 99, growing like grapes on the highway's vine. They didn't live in Amity, really. Their trailer was in a nearby pack of trailers and low-roofed bungalows that was an extra 15 minutes of driving, which made the whole endeavor half an hour each way. If she left straight from working at the school, she could browse the crooked shelves as long as she wanted and still be home before five. Dinner had to be started by five or else Dad would get the idea that he should make it, and a person could only eat so much overcooked spaghetti and microwaved meatballs before they decided that being home by five wasn't so bad. The risk was worth it though. Emily loved movies. She loved the stories, the music and she especially loved the Hollywood sets. With props, paint, and the right angles, a hot backlot could suddenly be anywhere in the world.

Today, she had left with plenty of time, but destiny apparently hated her taste buds. After a few minutes of putting off the inescapable, Emily clambered out of the car and opened up the trunk. Inside was a pile of PVC pipes and a bag of movies. There was a moment of wondering how far she could carry them together, but it passed quickly, and she grabbed the bag firmly in one hand and threw the trunk shut with the other. There was no way she was leaving these, not with *2001: A Space Odyssey* wrapped within the plastic.

"Watch for the match cut from the bone to the spaceship," Arnold, the video store owner, had told her. "Millennia skipped over in one cut; it's fucking awesome. Kubrick's something else, Ems. He's a god of the celluloid."

Arnold always talked like that; somewhere between Roger Ebert and a high school burnout. He dreamed of owning a theater, but all he could manage was an outdated video rental that made most of its money from the pornos. The backroom was sectioned off by a rainbow-colored bead curtain and guarded with a handwritten sign that read "18+ only." While Emily scoured through clamshells, reading the worn plastic cases, she would constantly hear the ding of the front door followed shortly by the clack of beads. What bothered her was how it disappointed Arnold. He once said that she was the only regular he wanted, and that gave her a sadness she couldn't put words to. As recompense, she put up with his nicknames and how he'd spoil movies to tell her about iconic shots.

The PVC was for Dad. He would be disappointed she left it behind, but it was just too much to juggle. Emily figured she had almost five miles to walk still, and it wasn't likely she could hitch a ride. She looked down the narrow strip of pavement in the wide, empty fields. On hot summer days, after the combines had scythed all the crops down, the road seemed as if it was drowning in the vastness of it all. The view made her stomach ache. The cheap plastic bag felt oily in her fingers and its contents felt oddly heavy. Emily gritted her teeth and started walking.

Ten minutes in, the rain began. She didn't notice the darkening skies, or the first few drops and it wasn't until one of the larger ones popped on her head that she realized what was happening. This fall had been hot and initially the cool rain was welcome against her dry, weary skin. But as it continued, dampness spread across her clothes and set in deeper. Suddenly a stab of panic hit her chest. What if the road washed out and she was swept away? The heavy clouds stretched too far to be a temperamental shower; their dark shape swelled endlessly above. There was no telling how long the storm might last. She quickened her pace and clutched the bag of movies tightly to her chest.

It was well past five when Emily got home and water had seeped completely through all of her clothes. She was wearing her favorite "Never Say Die" hoodie which was two sizes too big and would take days to dry completely. It had been a gift from Dad. When he gave it to her, he said they would take a trip to the coast and see *The Goonies* house in person. They never did.

Dad was standing in the doorway. His greasy black hair poked out of a red baseball cap, and he was struggling to push his arms through a trash bag wrapped around his torso. He had gotten his head through but couldn't find the other holes he had cut. Seeing her, he ran forward with no arms to balance and nearly toppled.

"Where the fuck have you been?" His voice let her know that he was more worried than angry. "I thought you got swept away in a flash flood or something."

"No, I'm alright."

"Come here." He broke one arm free and hugged her tightly. She could feel his rough chin on her forehead. "Thank god you're alright. I was just about to come looking for you."

"I'm fine Dad, just really wet. I need a shower."

"I'll bet. You go do that. Wait, did you get the pipes? Are they in the car?"

"Yes dad, I got them."

"Oh, perfect. Serendipity!"

"No, Dad, I got them, but the car broke down and I had to walk. The pipes are still in the car, like ten miles up the road."

Emily could see Dad fighting with whether he wanted to get them tonight, an untrackable calculus flitting behind his soft brown eyes. She left him like that and took a much-needed warm shower. Midway through, there was a knock on the bathroom door.

"We'll just get the pipes tomorrow once the rain stops," Dad shouted.

The next day the rain did not stop. From morning to night, the deluge continued. After the long, sodden walk the night before, she needed a personal day to stay home and watch movies. She called in to the school to let them know she was sick. Her work there was mostly helping with odd jobs and running the film projector when a teacher called out. There wasn't a lot of work besides the farms and vineyards, and this way she got to watch movies sometimes.

Dad took the day off as well. He served as the local handyman but was unable to repair anything significantly broken. Walking around, Emily would constantly recognize his work: a satellite dish held upright with duct tape and sticks, a porch step replaced with a skateboard, or a chair with a smaller stool for one of its legs. Their trailer was a museum of these peculiar repairs. She wished he had gone off to help someone patch a hole in their roof with an old car door or something. "There's no work more important than my daughter," he would say when she asked him if anyone had a job needing doing. The pipes almost drew him out, but the rain was pounding hard enough that he put it off one more day.

He always talked over the movies and Emily hated that. She would have to ask Arnold about the end of *2001* because of all the interruptions. He kept complaining about how confused he was and couldn't figure out why there was a strange baby on the screen. He asked her what it meant, but she had no answer because she hadn't been able to follow along with his incessant commentary. She wished she had an answer, so badly. She wanted to have a whole essay brimming in her throat, but his questions were like the plinking of rain on the roof, constant and leaving no room for her own thoughts.

Most of the neighborhood lived in narrow, squat houses that looked like trailers, but theirs was the only one with wheels. Not that it did any good as the tires were flat and sunk halfway into the earth. They had a cluttered living room that was also the kitchen and two sectioned off bedrooms at either end. Emily once overheard Mom call it ramshackle and the word stuck in her mind ever since. The rain drummed all day and long into the night.

Needing a break from home, Emily made the walk to the school the next day. She had a feeling that Dad would want to go get the pipes if she played hooky again. If she had to trudge through the rain anyways, the school was much closer than Stanley. All of the roads and lawns were covered with a thin film of water, making every street indefinite and endless. Emily's shoes couldn't hold up and her socks were quickly drenched. By the time she got to the school, her raincoat was starting to give out as well. Mrs. Randall, the second-grade teacher, was the only person at the school she considered a friend. She was writing a romance novel and dreamed of having it published someday. During the passing periods, she would tell Emily all about the latest sex scene she had written; going into every tawdry detail despite the fact that she had once been Emily's teacher. Emily was glad for it. She loved hearing about all the exotic locales and the complicated backstories of each character. As Mrs. Randall read, she'd try to picture the set, the costumes, the blocking. Emily didn't care for it today though, and interrupted Mrs. Randall as she was recapping how Heath and Amy ended up in the abandoned submarine.

"That rain sure is annoying, isn't it?" Emily asked suddenly

"I didn't really notice."

"Didn't notice? How could you not notice?"

"I mean, yea, I noticed it, but whatever, it's just rain. It rains all the time."

"Yea, but…I don't know. Feels different."

Two thirds of the class had called out with colds, so they made it a half day. Emily's socks were still wet as she stepped back out into the rain to walk home. When she reached their trailer, Dad was sitting in a small wooden dinghy with two oars propped in the oarlocks. He was swinging a hammer down beneath the rim of the boat.

"What are you doing Dad?"

"Fixing the boat we used to take over to Hagg Lake," he said through the nails held in his mouth. "If the water gets high enough, we can use it to go get the pipes."

"What do you even want them for?" she asked, entirely sick of the fucking pipes.

"Well, I didn't know before, but now I figure we could build a rain collector. Might as well make use of the weather we got."

A broad smile stretched across his face as he looked up at her from his work. She shook her head and went inside to put on dry socks. Dad scrambled out of the boat to follow her.

"Wait up, don't leave me out here," he called after her.

Each day the rain fell harder. Pools began to form in yards and the roads were almost knee deep now. It didn't run off or ruin the town, it just kept rising; spilling through cracks and permeating every inch of Amity. They had to move all the school classes into the gym, where the students could sit in the bleachers and stay dry. One of the teachers had a little boat with an outboard motor and went to town to buy extra ponchos for the teachers and kids. Dad tried to convince Emily to ask if they could use the boat to get the pipes. She said she would but never did.

A week passed with the constant grey sky, the ceaseless rain, and Dad's insistence all growing together. Even as it rained and rained and rained, Dad only seemed to care about the pipes. Finally, she decided that one terrible day was worth putting an end to the complaining and the pair began the long slog through the water and mud.

Dad rigged up an umbrella to his backpack and hovered close so that they could both be under it. The road was completely submerged by now, making each step an exhausting effort. It didn't take long for them to stray off and get lost. After an hour, they gave up on making it to the car and the rest of the day was spent finding their way home.

School was cancelled once the water reached past the kids' waists. No one seemed to mind. Mrs. Randall was even happy that she'd have more time to work on her book. Emily spent each day watching the same movies over and over. Days lost their meaning and instead she measured time in how often HAL shut down and how high the water rose. Each morning Emily would wake up to see it slightly higher than when she went to sleep. The first day that it rose high enough to be level with their trailer, Dad woke her up with excitement in his voice.

"Emily, wake up, c'mon wake up! I have a surprise for you."

Groggily she followed after him. "Couldn't it have waited?"

"Well, yes probably, but I had an idea last night and, well you'll see."

Stepping out of her room, Emily found a strange sensation between her toes. It was sand. Most of their kitchen floor had been covered by sand. The table was thrust aside, and two lawn chairs were planted in front of the wide-open door. Water lapped at the threshold, rising and falling like it did at the shore of a lake.

"Look!" Dad exclaimed with his arms held out. "Remember how we always wanted to take that trip to the beach? See the ocean and all that. Well, I decided to bring a bit of the ocean to us! What do you think?"

"Where did you get the sand?" was all she could think to ask.

"I had some lying around and figured there was nothing better to use it for."

Emily made them push the sand together to form a barrier at the door, much to Dad's dismay. That still didn't stop the water from coming in.

One month since the first day of rain, Emily woke up to the sudden shock of cold against her skin. She had rolled off of her bed and into the murky water that now flooded her bedroom. With a gasp,

Emily twisted upright, spitting out water and trying to find air. As her thrashing and panting calmed, she noticed a disposable camera floating on the surface of the water, its yellow body just barely bright enough to catch her eye in the dark.

Most of her room had been displaced by the water and the camera bobbed amongst the flotsam of clothes, posters and knick-knacks. She picked up the hollow body and looked at it. Dad had bought it for her after one of Mom's visits. Emily had been overcome by sadness, envy, anger, all crumpling together in her stomach. Then Dad walked up with the little black and yellow camera. He said to her that movies were just a bunch of pictures back-to-back, and that they could make one together. They did. It was short because almost half of the film didn't develop properly, but she used to sit and flip through the photos all day. Dad called it her directorial debut. The cheap plastic body felt like nothing now.

Emily had no idea where those pictures were, and they seemed more distant than ever. Now, each step Emily took was wet. Her clothes were never dry and her skin was in a constant state of prune. All the while, Dad sloshed around happily, always trying to figure out a way to reach the pipes or building some other contraption to make use of the weather.

It happened suddenly, even though she knew it was imminent. One night, the water threatened at the edge of her mattress when she went to bed, and as she was dreaming it crept up further. She didn't jolt awake this time, instead slowly coming to consciousness under-water. After a strange moment of stillness, she realized that her lungs were full and she was drowning. Emily sat up, heaving desperately, with no room for breath in her chest. She crawled forward and started to slam her stomach against the footboard. There were little ballerinas debossed into the wood. She used to stare at them and think about the time she visited Mom and they went to see *Swan Lake*. Mom asked if she wanted to take dance lessons, but that had been the last time Emily ever visited. The water came blasting out as she threw her guts against the ballerinas. Vomit accompanied the gush of water, until there was nothing left inside.

It was up past her hips as Emily stepped out of the bed. She slinked across her room, the surface of the black liquid rippling as she pushed through. In the main room, Dad was sleeping on the rickety kitchen table. His bed had submerged several days before. Emily stepped to the door of the trailer where she paused and watched her dad sleep. Turning back, she walked to the TV and grabbed her bag of movies from its top. Tucking them under her slick raincoat, she left the trailer with nothing else. The repaired dinghy was waiting. The odd wooden patches made her unsure of how long it could float.

The night was dark with clouds that let out a steady drizzle of rain. Lightning flashed and thunder rolled across the nearby hills. Emily couldn't see any stars in the blackness, but she continued to row towards her best guess at north. The rough oars tore at her hands and they quickly became sore. As she rowed away, Emily faced Amity. In the distance she could see the warm yellow glow of a single trailer turn on. She kept searching, looking to the sky for some shining star to guide her, but it never broke through the thick, rain-swelled clouds. So instead, she aligned that yellow glow in front of her and continued to row. The lightning would crash across the sky and light up the world for an instant. In that frame of a second she stared at Amity. With each flash it grew further away. Emily played these moments back-to-back in her mind and watched the picture they unfolded.

The Astronaut at the Mini Mart

Judith Mikesch-McKenzie

His father had taught him how to take care of a store, keeping
the windows & floor clean,
never let dust accumulate on any shelved items—and be
    sure all the light bulbs are working so
  that everything is not only clean, but bright.

Dad used to watch the launches with him, the same way sons
and fathers watch football teams and
cheer them—they'd comment on the countdown delays,
    and the merits and drawbacks of each
  landing site, and each pilot.

Until his father's own countdown ran out, and the store had
been sold to pay the hospital and
funeral bills, and he looks at the package in his hand,
    a cereal box with multi-colored stars
  around a fat rocket boosting its way

over the head of a wide-eyed bunny and he places it on the
shelf, his finger swiping to check for dust.

The Astronaut at the Mini Mart

He remembers the formula for calculating gravitational force,
      for figuring course correction
  and the calculus of launch parameters,

the velocity and thrust necessary for maintaining an orbit. He
stocks the shelves, wipes a few spots off the
windows, cleans and starts the coffee machine, and opens
      his till just before he turns over
  the open sign. Taking his spot behind the

counter, he looks out the window and up the hill, because it's
Tuesday and she always comes in on
Tuesdays, getting her coffee and her weekly pack of smokes,
      and smiling as she reminisces
  about his days in her class and he knows

she remembers the pictures of the Saturn V always glued to
his notebooks, and the sketches of planets
he drew next to the assigned calculations of force and motion
      and, rarely will ask him what he's
  done lately about his training, and he'll

take a breath, swallow hard, and smile at her as he
      pours her coffee.

On Being

Phillip Barron

Come home tired   walk in   legs sore   hungry
fold a sandwich and get one episode
deeper into the show I tell
no one I watch then scroll
and tap and read and when
I uncross one foot
has impressed the other. Whatever
pride I felt pedaling morning errands
is now a pink groove across a bulged vein
on a right heel and aching ankles. I slip
out the kitchen door to restore
focus in three dimensions of a small garden
and bees work the lavender like they never
stopped for lunch. I once read
that bees see colors on the violet end of the rainbow
best. One follows me to the hose and lands
on the nozzle after I refill the stone bath
for birds which leaks slowly after a late winter freeze.
A dry hot fire weather watch day and neither one
of us can drink enough water. I begin to see lavender
reflected in everything—droplets holding fast to leaves,
notebook ribbon, alumni t-shirt, pebbles underfoot,

the aching blue sky, fear of its vast emptiness,

the tip of the towhee's tail feathers

that steer the bird as it lands

in the tight space between scarcity and just enough.

Stacking Stones

David Sapp

Usually I am indifferent
Along this wooded path
Never taking much notice
Of the clumsy stacking of stones
By the anxious and overwhelmed
A self-soothing ritual
For the purpose of reflection
Mindfulness a trendy
Respite from apprehension
I prefer the undisturbed
A veristic placement
Of the chaos of nature
But this cairn differs
From most compositions
Someone has discovered
A massive block
Quarried hewn abandoned
Apparently useless
Over a century ago now
Overtaken by moss and lichens
And placed upon it
Five stones imperfectly

Chiseled round by glaciers
Spaced asymmetrically singly
And one upon another
At a particular moment
You will see if you are patient
The soft morning light
Illuminate the sculpture
In green chiaroscuro
Whatever the motivation
It is beautiful
Unexpectedly a comfort

Nature Journal

Michelle Boland

"One must have the bird in his heart before he can find it in the bush."
—John Burroughs

Ask if there hasn't been enough suffering,
and another bird leaves a feather in the yard.
Then two more, downy and white,
float, land on the planter wall below
where a Cooper's hawk has a mourning dove,
greige and full of the garden, pinned to the limb
highest in the sumac. It plucks feathers
away, cleans meat from the bone, eats bone.
Digests this other body.
It takes the hawk more than an hour
to complete its dissection.

And what does it say about me,
all this time keeping watch, a ghost
of birds in my window's periphery?
Fascination is a raw and confusing thing,
this mix of pity while admiring
what's done for survival,

the holding and severing, the hawk
scanning the yard for rivals between bites,
its white-tipped tail quivering
as though maybe ecstatic.

Owl Release

Dean Engle

We found the owl in the backyard one morning in November. My sister heard it first. That questioning cry, a screech with the intonation rising at the end. It lay on the grass, damp with dew and blood. Its feathers were ruffled and torn, matted with more blood. I had never seen an owl before, but I knew it shouldn't look like this. Owls are not meant to be seen in the daylight.

We ran to get our parents. Mother was still passed out on the couch. Father was in the kitchen, smashing an egg against the side of a pan. He startled as we ran in and the egg shattered, shell fracturing into the yolk. He turned and glared at us. We knew not to bother him when he was cooking, but it seemed like an emergency.

"What's happening," my mother asked, walking into the room, one hand pressed against her temple.

"There's an injured owl outside."

My father glanced toward my mother and then to us. He seemed so huge to us, a tall man, all jutting angles: the chin, the forehead, the knuckles. "Fine," he said. "I'll just have cold eggs." He flicked off the gas and grabbed a jacket from the kitchen chair.

My mother followed him, and we followed her.

The owl was still there, stunned and bleeding. It screeched as my father approached.

"Jesus," my father swore. "What happened to this thing?"

"It was another bird," my mother said. "A hawk or a falcon. That's a claw mark."

"No, it was a cat. Cat's have claws, birds have talons," he corrected.

"What do we do?" my sister asked.

"It's injured. We should put it out of its misery." He turned and walked back to the garage. He returned a moment later, a baseball bat hanging limply in his hand.

"Don't kill it, dad," my sister begged.

"This bird is hurt. It won't have a good life. I don't know what happened to it. Maybe it got pushed out too early, maybe a cat got it. On its own, it's dead."

"Don't Stephen," my mother said.

My father's knuckles tightened white around the bat. He drew a long inhale of breath, and then dropped the bat to the grass. "It won't live a good life. That's on you. Not me." He walked back into the house and made eggs for himself.

My mother had us get a carboard box, a towel, and a pair of scissors. With a lot of coaxing and a small stick, we got the owl inside the box. It stared up at us from inside the carboard, its beak opening and closing without sound. Its eyes were yellow and unfocused. For a horrible moment, I knew my father was right.

But that didn't stop my mother or my sister. They convinced my father, with a lot of grumbling and complaints about the price of gas, to drive us up into the hills. There was a wildlife museum that rehabilitated injured animals. My sister and I had been on a field trip once.

My mother and sister took the owl inside while I waited with my father in the car.

He drummed his fingers on the steering wheel and turned back to me. His eyes were red. "You know," he said. "Even if it survives. It'll never live a *wild* life."

A month later, we were back, the sun setting on the hills behind us. Huge oak and sycamore trees, their branches mostly bare, stretching above us. A ranger in khaki and a half a dozen volunteers stood at the front. At their feet sat pet-carrying cages, normally occupied by cats or small dogs. Inside these cages were owls.

The final rays of the sun set and the volunteers opened the containers. I could see our owl, hiding in the back of a pink dog crate. As the other birds moved forward and took flight, our owl stayed still. It didn't look like it could move. And then after a slow step, it wobbled forward and unfurled its wings. With a great flap, it rose, soaring up and out into the night.

"Well, I'll be dammed," said my father.

Years later, with both my parents gone, this is how I remember them, remember our family. My sister staring up at the sky, beaming. My father shifting from foot to foot, checking his watch. My mother wrapping her coat against her, the faintest smile on her lips. And me, huddled in the cold between them all.

My sister and I will sit with our tea sometimes and talk about the things we couldn't have talked about then—our father's anger and our mother's addiction. I wonder how we made it out, how we left their nest, scattered and bleeding. I wonder how much longer we can survive, if we can live a wild life ourselves.

Sooner or later, our conversation always turns to the owl. My sister will ask, nearly every time I see her, "Do you think he's still out there?" I do not know how long owls live. I've always been afraid to check.

On summer nights, lying in bed, the window open, I hear the questioning call. I wonder if it is our owl. And I return to that night, to a moment paused in time, our family preserved like a picture postcard before the gentle *whoo* fades to silence and cicadas.

Reckless We Love Ourselves

John Blair

Reckless we love ourselves for as long
as we may live, love the mud-slick slopes
in the forests of down and down and more

down where our aspirations like saplings
grow, where stumps will someday squat
maimed & fat with old sap, ready to burn

until nothing's left but bewilderment
and gouts of ash that fall with the rain
and drown, though a few sad coals

might still startle up now and again
when the wind freshens, when the thunder
grinds its birthing hips and the fires

that smolder in heartwood that's been
hardened by the sums of outrages and years
sparkle in a breeze like fields of hearths,

like little fox eyes, like fists holding flickered
stars inside or the "you are here" on maps
of churches and ruins that we have made

with our own busy hands to show where
all the seeds are laid, waiting to be split open
by the flames, the spots where each sprout

will begin to finger apart the loam
of the muddy altars down which we slide
like houses offered up by burned-over

Montecito mountainsides where something
still kindles borrowed, something still kindles
blue, fierce enough to hurt, to make raindrops

skitter like sweat on a griddle,
like blood, like the gumdrop souls
of mice and children sizzling reckless

in the palms of our bare hands
right down to the wailing heartwood
till there's nothing left to burn.

The Staircase

Judith Mikesch-McKenzie

i. The Widow's Helix
she never told her daughters to be tough,
but she trained them to be

rebel, devoted, religious , dreamer, full of
bitterness, holder of a quiet,
never-articulated resentment for life as
a woman,

she
never
surrendered—

true, sometimes they'd find her curled up in
a corner of the basement, blank, staring,
breath labored and sometimes explosive

the ones who found her never panicked,
or ran for help, because they
knew in their cells, in their very DNA ,
that they should leave her be
and she would come back, like the tide

ii. The Factorization of Plasma

we are mostly water, with much that swims in our
      blood—cells white and red, antibodies that defend
us, oxygen that fuels our days

everything that circulates through us moves like currents
      in the ocean, like the tide, like salmon who know in
their blood how to swim home, like how we know that
      resistance is the cause of drowning in calm water, and
how we know that the best choice is to simply lay back
      and float, embracing rain and river that feel nearest
to who we are, even though our tears are the precise
      measure of the oceans

we are clear water, our salt tears a release from
      oxygen and a surrender to the stillness
of floating along a waterway, the quiet pace
      and peace of surrender to our own

iii. the weight that is displaced

I knew that my sister's eyes were closed tight,
      she couldn't bear anything touching
her eyes, but mine were wide open, staring
      through the clear water at the rocks
and soil on the lake bottom far below, and the
      fish that seemed to be drifting by as though
in air. We floated side by side. the mountain sun
      a warm brick on our backs, and I am lost
in the beauty of the wide space beneath me

that somehow holds me aloft, and my sister,
eyes squeezed tight, waits to hear our mother
noticing her two daughters, limp, motionless
and floating face down on the water.
The thing is...she never did.

iv. the capacity for blunders

the matrix of life is water—our DNA is
coated with water that prevents
that famous double helix from dissolving
water is our mother, our home,
and somehow the
way to vanquish the barriers of

time, finding parallel lives for each of
us through the tides and
currents that connect everything
through micro-portions of our DNA
that we leave with our mothers, who
carry it in their water-blood for
their entire lives, so

that somehow, we exist with them as
we exist now. We sit here, feeling
ourselves sundered and
sovereign, while all the while,
deep in our blood, we exist elsewhere,
in her blood

v. the language of our molecules
I used to dream about those long dark stairs
that led to the basement where she
hid sometimes—steep and
unstable, built in another century,
and when I was not on the stairs looking
for her, those stairs felt
like a time machine, like I was not here
and now, but here long ago, not me,
growing up now, but in this
house when she grew up here,
young, cocky, prone to aiming her
bicycle through pools of wet
mud on purpose, and then here again,
decades later, hiding in the basement
to struggle with…what?

is it possible that, there
on the basement floor, she was simply
overwhelmed with our presence, her own
fears, pains, and losses amplified
by ours that swim in her blood, overwhelming her like a
tidal wave, so that all she could do was float,
eyes tight, until the water receded

Watching Others

Ty Zhang

Did you know?
That there are really those among us unafraid to live?
Who know how to do things like to sing and to dance,
To speak and act accordingly,
And to dare?
Is it that their lungs extract courage from the atmosphere—
Or do they simply require none
Whereas I need a dose just to breathe?

Perhaps doubt does not chase them through the days.
Perhaps, like for the rest of us, it does,
Though they defend against it
Reciting something talismanic like:
Better to be a failure than a coward.
What if they're right?

I want to be like them—
To drink my fill of life.
It's funny
How paralyzing envy can be.

Tit for Tat

Jack D. Harvey

She laughed
and her noble Roman nose
appropriated her mouth;
drinking technicolor cocktails
at some fancy downtown restaurant
I smiled, adding a touch of horse
to my mien
and motored on, told the waiter
to bring another round.

Among mechanical goldfish
flitting sandwiched in the glass walls,
the live lobsters
lined up in tanks,
we drank more and more
and, what the heck,
for the reckoning to come
we moved to champagne;
she laughed again, so heartily
her décolleté dress slipped down in front,
revealing *de trop* the twin slopes
of her bastioned embonpoint.

Ha, ha, heh, heh, huff, huff
I chuffed like a toy
steam engine, trying my best
to get to my point
before she got to hers
and quicker on the draw
in the nick of time succeeded.

You stole my father's love,
I told her,
stole like a thief in the night
in the dark of his bedroom
did the deed,
bed-playing him
to a fare-thee-well,
draining him like a succubus,
a night creature
like Lilith in the Bible.

Her breasts and forehead glistening
smooth in the candlelight,
no, no, nyet, nyet
she gaily chaffed,
wagging her finger at me,
not at all, at least
not only that way.
I loved your father
sincerely, passionately,
through all the stolen days

we kept together, loved him
till the day he died;
I love him still,
sadly, longingly,
a long-gone wraith,
a reminder of long-ago happiness.

You lie, you trollop,
leaning in close
over the table,
that's not the switch,
you witch, you bitch,
I don't take
your lover's refrain
to give me enlightenment,
to show the truth
to close the door
on what you did,
invading home and hearth
bringing shame and dishonor.

I loved my father
bearing the weight of his sins
like patient Atlas,
father and son
a bond of blood;
not a whore like you
feeding his baser needs
with your tricks of the trade,

memories of former clients,
former favors
running through your head.

She smiled hard and furious,
hard white Kabuki face
revealing nothing but disdain;
in a moment composed,
sitting up proud and straight
started to speak.

Do I care, she said,
your misplaced judgment
does you no good, serves no purpose.
You said your piece
but told me nothing;
a selfish son's hurt feelings.

Now it's my turn
to close this out
take my leave of you
and your filial trumpeting.

Yes, I fucked your father.
So what?
In his benighted life
even for a short time
I made him happy as a king.

Square the tab
and go to the devil
with your moral self-indulgence,
your blessed ignorance
of the hard facts.

Do you think you knew your father
better than I?
If I told you what I knew about him?

There's more to a man
than his sons, his hearth, his home.

Poor soul, you owe me
more than you think.

Expulsion

John Cullen

The Devil crooned
country music, and God
realized he required
a new tune, tasking
Adam and Eve: birth a beat.

Strums and fiddles,
for centuries, but God
didn't hear a single,
just the usual: Holy, Holy, Holy,
figs, light, forbidden fruit.

"Bust loose! Make a Banger!
Shake me to the bone!"
So Adam and Eve too
screamed, then hid smiles
when God puckered.

"Fuzz this bitch,
kick in the speakers!"

Adam snarled, volume
squealing. It was
the feedback he needed.

So the band toured. God
stayed home, listening
to oldies and cursing.
The Devil snickered
at his mirror.

Generational Lack

Gabryél Grimm-Goretez

I think of you a lot at night
Louder voices insist you wouldn't be proud
But I remember you
Fiery, crackling like lightning, but you were so inviting
I can still feel the echoes of your thunder
And I know that I don't ever have to wonder

A Postcard Poem from *To Punani Camp*

samodH Porawagamage

My Hope,

Sarath ayya and his son Sahan came when I was with Niduk by the stream today. They carried Niduk to the middle of it and started giving him swimming lessons. Our son took to the water like a little merman, going up and down like a ball. Not once they had to teach the same thing to him. I anyway guarded the downstream out of abundant caution. He was in the water for over an hour and I worried about him catching a cold. Out of the water, he could barely walk. Now, he's practicing new techniques of his own in the bed. I won't take him swimming on my own, though. We should never forget what happened to our best swimmers! No need to count, but the war, reckless swimming, and pesticides are responsible for about the same number of untimely deaths in the village—also in my family. Yet all the talk is about constructing an electric fence to contain the elephants! And the officials are coming every week to buy people's chena lands for nothing. The government cares more about the elephants than us, even though the UNP is its main opposition.

Wife

Through the Pillars, By the Tracks

Shawn Schenck

—*for the Cathlascans of Upper Chinook*

The house had three rooms, no more than the duplex they'd just left, but it was a *house*. Moving schools would be nothing new, but this time was the strangest. In Gladstone, middle school started in the fifth grade, unlike many other school districts. Simon had just grown comfortable with the odd dynamic, only to return to elementary school in Clackamas the next year and re-graduate to middle school the year after that. A back-and-forth that cost him his only friend and the confidence he needed to make more.

Simon's new room was more spacious than the one in the duplex. His small bed and dresser left a vacant space that would eventually house piles of clothes, discarded snacks, and topical ephemera. But not now. Now, he had his bed, dresser, white noise machine, comic books, and alarm clock. The room was wedged between his mother's and younger sister's, across from a closet and bathroom, tiling the hallway with doors.

He sat alone, flipping through the pages of a comic book. Cassie, his mom, approached his door, hiding her guilt for pulling him out of another school and taking him from his best friend, Josh. She remembered how electric they were together, how sweet he sounded saying "*best* friend."

"Simon," she tried not to startle him. "Honey."

"Huh," he mumbled, twisting to see her.

"Why don't you go out and explore? Get to know the area."

"Because that's bor..." the words trailed from him, stopped by his mother's response.

"No excuses." Her left eyebrow raised in its knowing way.

The house sat at the end of the cul-de-sac, in the center of its bulbous turnaround. The narrow, straight path did little to satisfy his curiosity. He could hear his sister's laughter from the backyard fading in the distance behind birdsong and static.

Testing the limits of his eleven-year-old freedom, Simon galloped to the end of the lane and glanced, first to his left and then to his right. The street at the end of the cul-de-sac would fluctuate with intense bouts of traffic, tying two freeways together.

It stood still.

Warmed by the gaze of the August Sun, Simon crossed the street, twisting his head back and forth. His rubber soles clapped against the concrete before reaching the other side of the road. Easing himself down the sidewalk, Simon passed cul-de-sac after cul-de-sac, growing more unhappy with each discovery. *Is it all the same?*

The thought was gone as quickly as it came. Slowing to a stop, Simon stared at a pair of white stone pillars. Pillars that had lived on the land far longer than the surrounding neighborhoods. Rudimentary brick walls grew out of the columns, protecting the dirt path between them. The trail was hidden from the Sun by a bigleaf maple and its towering canopy of branches and leaves. *It looks like a bridge*, he thought. *But where does it go?*

His right foot following the left, Simon entered the darkening tunnel. The brick walls beside him stood eight feet tall, consisting of various-sized stones and tightly packed mud. As he continued, the light from the world behind him faded. Ahead, Simon could see that the path dipped into a decline. Reaching the start of the stoop, Simon could see over the descending walls, their abrupt end at the bottom of the hill, and the dense forest that engrossed him. He followed the trail to the end, continuing through to the clearing in the woods. To his surprise, the path led to gleaming silver train tracks. The tracks sat atop a long groove of gravel, raised from the ground like an overstimulated vein. *Maybe the land is angry.*

Simon glanced, first to the left, then to the right. The woods surrounded the path, dense with western redcedar, sword fern, and Indian plum. He considered the crossroad and looked back to the trail behind him. His curiosity had peaked, but the thought of his mother worrying stopped him in his tracks. *Get to know the area.* Her words echoed through his mind.

The boy began to his right, stepping on the planks that tiled the irritated land between the iron tracks. *One, two, three*, he counted. The rocks between the planks began to fade from their uniform grey to a sepia-tinted brown. *Eight, nine, ten...* Simon looked up, eyes darting from left to right, down to up. A towering wall of trees stood before him, stopping him in his tracks.

Simon took another step, rolling his foot on a foreign object. Falling to the ground, he braced himself for the cold punch of the rail. Instead, he landed in the grass, sending a soft cloud of dust into the air. Grass that hadn't been there before. The tracks were gone. He looked back to reassure himself that the trail he'd followed still existed. Only grass, surrounded by dense forest. *What happened?* Surprised and suddenly aware of a calming, distant whir, he sat still. A nearby river purred its white noise, reminding Simon of the white noise machine he uses to sleep. Looking back to his feet, Simon found the object responsible for his fall; the bones of a long-dead animal. *A wolf*, he considered. The bones were bigger than any he'd ever seen, bigger than the roadkill he would casually avoid when waiting for the school bus or walking to the park with his mom and sister. Wiping himself of dirt and grass, Simon stood and reconsidered his surroundings.

"Hello," his soft voice barely breached the sounds of the surrounding woods.

A nearby tree branch moaned in response, swaying with the wind. *No, there's no wind.* Simon's uncle told him about cougars and bobcats, how they hide in trees, waiting to pounce on their prey. His heart raced, beating his body into a vibration. *I should have gone back. I want to go back.* Hoping to get a visual of the beast on the branch, Simon focused his eyes in the direction he'd heard the sound.

Which branch?

Time seemed to stop.

Which branch?

The forest stood still.

That one?

A bead of sweat swept down Simon's face from his forehead. His hot atom eyes swept from branch to branch, retracing their path in uncalculated jags. They stopped, pausing on the source of the moving limb. A pair of glowing ruby eyes watched from within the brush of leaves. Simon sat frozen, watching the Watcher. The eyes faded into the shrouded darkness, followed by an urgent crack and weighted *thump*. The Watcher launched itself from the branch and landed on the soft dirt floor. Simon slowly backed away, convinced he'd be more vulnerable with his back to the predator, his *I can't see you, you can't see me* logic taking full control.

From a nearby copse, a cluster slightly disassociated from the rest of the forest, the Watcher revealed himself, his sandy brown and white coat a blur against the wood and dirt. *A Coyote.* Simon recognized the rough similarities between it and the cartoon he sometimes watched with his sister. *Thank God you're not carrying dynamite.* The thought flashed through his mind. He knew his sister would have thought it was funny.

Simon and the Coyote stood still, eyes locked in anticipation. For a moment, Simon wondered if the Coyote was really there or if he'd hit his head on the track when he fell and had been dreaming the whole thing. He cringed at the thought of brain damage, of being hurt and alone in the middle of the forest.

The Coyote's sudden movements swept Simon's thoughts away. To his surprise, the Coyote seemed to lose interest in him and began to walk away. He watched its feathery tail sway to the left and right as it slowly disappeared into the trees. The pressure in his chest relieved itself, and he could breathe again. A pang of anxious curiosity overtook the boy. He followed the Coyote trail, only made aware of his own movements by the sounds of twigs cracking beneath his shoes. The darkness of the forest made itself known, crept its cold chill up the boy's arms and neck. He tried his best to ignore the shiver.

A wall of light appeared through the thinning trees. The once calming whir of the river grew into a steady growl. Simon passed through the last of the trees, glaring into the light as his eyes adjusted. The river foamed white with its rapid stream, dancing and splashing over the rocky bed beneath. Birdsong briefly pierced the white noise.

He's gone.

Simon glanced around, scanned the rocky shores on either side of the river, and took inventory of the parallel forest line. The liveliness of the river emphasized the deadly stillness of the world around him. *I'm lost.* His stomach floated in the bile of fear that raged within him.

A familiar moan caught Simon's attention, the sway of a nearby branch. Simon found the source of the sound, the Coyote hanging in the open sky above the river. It watched the river beneath it, the branch swaying under its weight. The boy was mesmerized, caught up in his curiosity.

Ignoring him, the Coyote gazed into the river as though waiting for some signal unknowable by people. A language that belonged to the land, to the creatures and critters living among the bush and brush. The Coyote found its signal, sprang back on the branch, and began shaking itself. The boy anticipated long trails of water droplets to rain into the river below, acclimating themselves with subtle ease. But the Coyote wasn't wet, and water didn't rain from its dense fur coat.

Instead, a silky flow of coarse sand poured from the coyote into the river with a fury, splashing the boy on the shore. Simon stood still, frozen in awe, and watched the impossible deluge of sand pouring from the animal. A great, dark shadow grew from within the river, spreading to the opposing bank. Growing and growing. Simon watched the shadow penetrate the surface of the river, revealing its true form. The sand had grown into a dam bridging the banks on either side.

The Coyote dropped to the shore and looked at Simon with a new expression: curiosity. Without looking away, the Coyote began across the newly formed bridge. Simon followed, unsure of how he was meant to respond or what the animal could be trying to tell him. His decision proved correct as the Coyote broke its gaze and maintained its gait. Together, they entered the opposing forest. Deeper and deeper, they steadied themselves into the trees. The Coyote led the boy past termite-infested fallen oak, patches of fern, and an owl that Simon thought looked very concerned.

They stopped at the base of a nondescript great maple oak, similar to the one Simon had seen at the pillars. *The pillars*, he thought, secretly hoping the Coyote had been somehow leading him back to them. Without looking to check on the boy, the Coyote launched itself up the tree in a flash of brown and white. Simon smiled to himself, wondering if the Coyote might be hiding some dynamite in his fur. A sudden, quiet *crack* broke the boy's thought. The sound of an egg falling to the floor. The sounds that followed, of expanding wood, trees bending against themselves in explosive winds, floorboards flexing beneath a child's weight in the night, reverberated from the other side of the tree. The *crack* of twigs followed, growing louder with each step.

A fur-robed figure appeared from around the tree. His robe was the same brown and white as the Coyote he'd been following.

"Wh-ho—" Simon choked on his words.

"Why are you here?" The Man asked.

"I-I came through the pillars."

The Man glared back in response, attempting to decode the child's words. "You don't belong here. You must go back."

Simon looked around, searching for some sign of an exit.

The Man continued, "You aren't safe."

His warning sent a chill up Simon's spine and erected the hairs on the back of his neck. "What does that mean? Not safe from what?" Simon stepped back.

"The *Glutton*."

A belted kingfisher wailed in the distance.

"What's the Glutton?"

"A giant beast," the Man began. "It's like a man, but not. The size of two bears. His hunger is insatiable, and his thirst…," he stopped, recognizing the child's innocent eyes. "He cannot be stopped, so you must go."

"Can you help me?" Simon stood out of place within the labyrinthine sea of green and brown, the fear he wore on his face a beacon of vulnerability. He realized how lost he truly was.

Simon watched the Man as he stood in silence, evaluating the situation.

"Come with me."

The Sun moved through the sky, shadows creeping in an eternal game of hide-n-seek. The forest whispered its familiar gossip of squirrels and rabbits, falling branches, and thriving winds. The subtle patter of their footsteps became another instrument in the summer song. A familiar whir of white noise grew louder with each step, a raging river in the near distance.

Walking on a lightly worn trail, surrounded by tall grass, the Man led Simon. He tried his best to answer the boy's questions, offering him salmon to distract from the more complex probes. He told the boy, "Call me Talla." Simon introduced himself, embarrassed that he'd completely forgotten to mention his name. Talla told Simon of Tomanowos, a sacred rock with limitless power, the answer to Simon's predicament. Simon asked if there were roadrunners in the wild. Talla wasn't sure what a *roadrunner* was.

"How far to tom-e-no-us?" Simon asked, sounding out the word as best as he could remember it.

"Not far," Talla answered through a smile.

A guttural squeal pierced the calm, paralyzing Simon with fear. Talla craned his neck to face the direction of the death call.

"The Glutton," Talla whispered. "We must go. Now."

Simon and Talla broke into a sprint. Sweat beaded and trailed down the boy's face hiding his tears. "Don't look back," Talla's voice was muffled by the heavy beat of racing blood through Simon's ears. The edge of a new forest grew nearer, taller. Passing through a gate of oak, another squeal exploded from behind them, much louder than the one before. Simon cried out in fear against his will, horrified by the impending threat. Talla reached back, grasping the boy's hand, and pulled him along. Trees flashed by in quick blurry succession like frames of damaged film. *Just like film*, he thought. *Just a movie. It's not real.*

"We're close," Talla whispered, breaking Simon's mantra.

A third squeal shattered their concentration, loud enough to leave their ears ringing. Simon couldn't feel himself shaking, shivering, passively moving forward. The forest suddenly broke, revealing an open ring of grass, light shining down like rays of gold. In the center of the ring sat Tomanowos; a 10-foot tall stone, beautifully eroded from its remarkable life.

"What do we do?" Simon asked, fear leaking from his every word.

It was too late. The trees behind them, posts of the stone's natural fence, bent out and away, revealing their stalker. A massive beast with vaguely human features stood and watched. Its shoulders bore bear snouts that stretched into hanging robes of fur. Large mounds of flesh showed through the tattered robes, scarred and flexed. Its trunk-like legs fit tightly into the bear's feet, clawing at the ground beneath. Its cheeks swelled out beside its jutting jaw, hiding its shark eyes and displaying its gnashing teeth.

"The Glutton," Simon managed a whisper.

Talla began toward the beast, carefully placing each foot. He shouted words Simon hadn't ever heard, collections of unfamiliar sounds. The Glutton's eyes stayed locked on Simon, watching the boy as a cat watches a mouse. Talla picked up his pace but the monster dashed toward Tomanowos, toward the boy. Talla approached it, but the Glutton knocked him away with the back of his hand, sending him sailing through the air. Simon stood frozen, watching as the monster got closer and closer.

A hard surface pressed against his back, Simon pressed himself into Tomanowos, unable to take control of his body. The Glutton closed in, pounding his feet against the grassy earth, snarling and gnashing. Simon closed his eyes, felt himself lift from the ground, and waited for the horror that followed. The Glutton squealed, again, from below. Simon opened his eyes and looked around. He was hovering. Looking down, he saw the angry beast growing angrier and angrier.

"I'm flying!" Simon shouted with glee.

"No," Talla answered from behind. "Stay up here."

Talla pulled Simon up to the top of Tomanowos, to temporary safety. The stone wouldn't budge despite the Glutton's many attempts to tackle it. Talla jumped to the ground, finally gaining the monster's attention. He continued shouting words Simon didn't know, running in circles around the beast. Simon watched in awe, excited by the thrill of being saved. And safe. Their fur flashed against each other in sporadic flashes, two bears herded by a lone coyote.

The Glutton broke their celebration, reached for Talla, and tore him from the ground by his throat. Simon watched his friend suspended in grim levitation. Panic flooded the boy, followed by action. Simon leaped from Tomanowos, landing in a roll before breaking into a full sprint. The surrounding ring of trees broke where the monster came through. The massive trail the beast had torn into the forest revealed the way back. Simon neared the swaying, broken branches, the chewed-out trunks. He stopped abruptly and scanned the ground. Wooden shrapnel littered the grass, a hodgepodge of browns amongst a green canvas.

Perfect, the boy thought, lifting a fallen branch from the ground. The broken end splintered into a sharp point. Simon held it out with both hands, sharp end forward, and charged the beast. His feet pistoning beneath him, seconds turned to minutes, infinities living and dying between each footfall. The Glutton turned at the sound of the boy's heavy breathing and watched as his prey jolted toward him in a fury.

Talla fell to the ground, fought for his breath, and grasped at his throat. The blackness faded from his vision. The Glutton stood beside him, tall and still. Simon no longer held the branch, though his hands hung around it waiting for it to drop. Attempting another squeal, the monster screwed up its face and released a pathetic whine, before falling to the ground. Simon and Talla watched in disbelief at their success. Simon's success. Talla stood and put his hand on Simon's frail shoulder.

"You saved me," Talla broke the silence.

Simon looked at him, accepted the truth of the statement, and nodded.

"Are you ready to go home?"

Simon nodded, again.

Simon and Talla approached Tomanowos, dwarfed by the giant stone. Standing before it, Talla looked to the boy with reverence.

"Okay," Talla began. "But before you go..." He picked at his wrist and loosed a thin braided leather bracelet. He took the boy's hand and slipped the bracelet over his fingers. "This is for you. To remember."

"How could I forget," Simon fell into Talla and began to cry.

Talla hugged the boy until his small shoulders stopped heaving and the tears dried up. Tomanowos began to glow, brighter and brighter with each second.

"Goodbye, Simon."

"Goodbye, Talla."

The light overwhelmed Simon, a hot white flash too bright to see. He stood in blinding whiteness, completely aware of Talla's fading embrace. The fading embrace of the world. Simon stood alone in the bright white nothingness, closed his eyes, and imagined the pillars. The distant cry of a belted kingfisher pierced his thoughts.

Eyes open, he saw the pillars, a world he recognized just beyond them. He was seeing them from the other side, facing away from the stooping path he remembered following. Simon passed through the pillars and flashed down the sidewalk in a flurry. He passed the boring cul-de-sacs and stopped across from his new home. Looking left and then right, Simon sprinted across the street and back to his house. He exploded through the front door with excitement, throwing his arms around his mother and sister.

Simon passed the pillars for years, placing mental police tape across them. His memories were equally frightening and invigorating, of exploring, making a friend, and nearly being eaten alive; feelings he couldn't quite explain, nor would he be able to if he could. No one would believe him. Why should they? He could hardly believe it himself, some days deciding it had only been a dream, that he had only hit his head and hallucinated. The mindset would quickly fade at the impossibility of his leather bracelet. The expertly tanned hide that Talla had braided into a thin band.

Some years later, after the advent of the internet, Simon would find himself reading about Tomanowos: the Willamette Meteorite, and about Tallapus turning himself into the coyote. He read as much as he could, falling deeper and deeper in love with the stories of the Upper Chinook. But they weren't just stories. They were the truth of the people.

Childhood

Bradley Samore

I thought if I kept folding it like a piece of paper
it would disappear and leave me alone
but it only got thicker

----

the dust is gathering
the silverfish feasting

----

each time I take an item out of the drawer
I wrap a new context around its old one
I'm not sure if I can undo this

I thought one room was a field
but there always seems to be another door
I wonder what's outside

I make the mirrors face each other

----

derelict rooms
please don't forget about me

I peel my scabs and lay them before me
and still I don't get my wounds

I show my passport
this led to this led to this

I quilt myself
or do the patches constitute me

---

outside the last door
rain
applauding its own arrival

Sincerely, the Trees in the Park

—after David Hernandez's "Sincerely, the Sky"

Vivienne Popperl

Yes, we see you circling,
face upturned, peering

into our leafy bustle in summer
through our bare branching arms

in winter. We see you marveling
at our shimmer and pulse in the fall,

our yellow fluff and feathery greens
in spring. What are you hoping

to learn from our hawk harboring
crow seesaws, our squirrel scooted trunks?

You've walked here for years. You know
how we fling sideways in the wind,

bow down and break under ice. How,
caressed by rain and mist, we gleam in the sun.

How often we've observed you, steps
rapid, shoulders hunched, fists

jammed into pockets. To you, we are
background, rustle and slip, whisper

and crisp, trace scent of crushed leaves
and loam. Remember, we put everything

into reaching for sunshine, for fog.
Don't hold back. Keep reaching

toward the light.

A Postcard Poem from *To Punani Camp*

samodH Porawagamage

My Heartbeat,

How could you tell I have a poet's heart? It's a strange thing to say to someone who has never written a verse...All I do is pour myself into postcards like a monsoon that floods the roadside puddles, without control or style. Some days I wonder if it's my worrying you're in danger versus sensing you're safe that begets these words. They are for me as much as for you, as I navigate the not-having of having. When I worry about not having, southbound breezes blow your scent my way. I'm not superstitious, but it's heretical to mistrust mother nature! I dream about perfection too: having you here with me and not having poetry at all. In a world without suffering, who needs poetry? Maybe poetry exists to make the world more bearable, and then disappear.

Your Monsoon Heart

The Sorrows of Kuan Hsiu (832–912)

Bruce Parker

He wrote of a hundred sorrows
without naming one:

parents returned to the earth;
daughter long ago parted from;

two sons' hardship and danger defending the borders;
infant still in its cradle, still;

the first and the five thousandth word of the Confucian classic,
memorized, the doorway to the scholar class;

emperor like a load of wood on an old man's back;
dogs and children that chased a ragged wanderer;

loneliness in winter mountain passes;
fishermen taken by a flood;

brackish water to drink, or none at all;
moonlight on a stone with no name;

sitting zazen
while ill;

the goose that pecked, the chicken that would not die,
the pig that cried when pierced by the butcher's knife;

the headache after wine
and the woman left behind,

her own sorrows too new,
her tears and lies;

cold Autumn winds
that drive dry leaves along;

the things he could not remember,
the things he could not forget.

Unity

Sharon Morris

My husband went hunting last spring. His buddies Kenny and Derek came over one night and asked if he wanted to go for wild turkey. They planned to go to a stretch of forest between Unity and Prairie City. Bill thought about it, kicked a loose board on our porch, then said he'd like to go. He'd never been hunting up there. Usually, he went south to Juniper or Steen's Mountain. He asked if they'd be camping out and they said sure, nothing like a couple of spring nights under the stars, right? He gave them one of his slow smiles and said right. I brought out a round of beers to celebrate. Don't worry Kelly, Derek said as we clinked our bottles, we'll bring him home safe and sound.

A few days later, Bill started assembling supplies on our living room floor. He'd put one thing down, like his sleeping bag or a Value-Pack of jerky, consider it, then either leave it there or put it away and lay out another thing. I'm no hunter but by the end of the evening even I could see he had assembled a masterful assortment of gear; sleeping bag, camo, long johns, binoculars, his Browning Gold Light, which was for turkey, and his Marlin 1984 for bear, but only if they ran into one, because the main point was turkey.

I met Bill my senior year of high school, right after I moved out of my mom's place and in with my uncle. When I first started hanging out with Bill and his friends, I felt like I'd fallen into the middle of a Pendelton catalog. Because of my living situation, I was always on edge back then. They were the complete opposite. They were calm and wholesome and smelled like grass clippings. After school, we'd walk through fields and stare at sunsets. Or, we'd sit around campfires and tell slow jokes. To join in the fun, I'd drop in conversational nuggets about things I'd learned that day, like did you know butterflies taste with their feet? They'd blink and smile and say, feet! then laugh. It wasn't mean. None of them had a mean bone in their entire bodies. I think they just didn't get most of what I said. Still, it sure was nice being part of a group like that, you know?

Bill was gone for three days. The night he got back, we sat outside and talked about his trip. He kept saying how awesome it was, even though they didn't get a turkey. While I watched green lacewings dance around our porch light, he said the pine needles made a sound like bells and the juniper tasted briny. He told me that one morning he got up early, stood by a lake, and drank the purest air he's ever had. He kept mixing up taste and smell and sound, but it all made sense in a funny way that I liked. It's like he fell head over heels in love up there, but in a non-threatening way.

After he'd been back a few days, I noticed he got quieter than usual and he's never been a big talker. He'd sit on our porch for hours, feet on the railing, drinking Gatorade, and eating creamed corn straight from the can. Sometimes, on his days off, he'd be in the same place as when I left for my job. Usually, he's all about doing what needs to be done, like fixing the fence or helping Mr. Farley with his cows. I didn't mind him taking the time to sit all day, it just wasn't like him to get all dreamy.

Other things too. Like one morning when I opened the drapes, he winced and said the light hurt his eyes, even though we hadn't been drinking the night before. Loud noises started to bother him too and his skin started to feel weird, sort of...felty maybe? He's always been husky, but when I put my arms around him at night, he felt denser, meatier.

I figured maybe he caught something on his trip, so I started googling forest/hunting diseases. I sat at our kitchen table and put together a spreadsheet of thirty-two possible options, from Babesiosis to Sarcoptic Mange, but nothing really seemed to fit his symptoms; dreaminess, sensitivity to light and noise, felty skin, meatiness. When I asked him questions to narrow it down, like was he bitten by a tick or exposed to any deer urine, he said no, nothing like that, he felt fine. Never better in fact.

After a couple of weeks, I decided to call Derek's girlfriend to see if we could organize a pool night at RJs. I told her it was so the guys could reminisce about their trip, but really it was to see if Kenny and Derek were acting as weird as Bill. We drank too much, we always do, but this time it affected Bill way more than normal. It's like his lips forgot how to shape sounds and his words came out all flubbery. Then, when he tried to step back and line up a shot, his legs kind of stuck together and he fell backwards into a bunch of high tops. I mean, it was really funny, but looking back, all I can see is Kenny's red face, mouth wide open, laughing. Bill chuckled along as we helped him to his feet, but I could tell he was confused. He's always been the steady one.

For most of my life, I've felt like it's my job to figure things out and fix whatever is broken. I guess that's why I like research so much; you never know when a piece of information can get you out of a tough spot. But it makes me restless, you know? All that information out there in the world; I want to run to it, swim through it, trace it to its source. Bill has always been the calm to my storm. He is happy where he is. He never questions. He just takes care of me and lets things unfold the way they will. I've tried to be more like that, but it never works for long. Which means, basically, that I still kept a close eye on Bill that spring and summer. I knew something was going on, I just didn't know what.

Most days, he was fine and I could pretend that we were back to normal. Other days, he'd do something strange, like laugh at something I couldn't hear or touch something I couldn't see. If I told him I was worried about him, he'd wrap me up in his arms and say everything is okay, Kelly. Sometimes that still worked and I'd sink back and drift off to sleep. I used to sleep for *hours* when we first met, right after he stepped into the mess that was my life. Other times though, when I'd ask him what was going on and he'd try to fold me up in a big, warm, manly embrace, I'd struggle out of his arms and say come on, honey, there's calm and then there's this.

Summer slowly turned over to fall. One evening on my way home from work, I stopped to pick up a few things for dinner. Since Bill was still having trouble with loud noises, I was cruising the produce bins looking for non-noisy vegetables, when a faint scent tugged at me, like a memory of a memory of something I once knew. I picked up an acorn squash and sniffed that, then some spinach, then finally I hit the portobellos and bingo! the smell was super familiar; a little like dirt, a little sweet, a bit like flour. I swear it was the same smell as Bill's side of the couch. This finally felt like a clue I could use, so I leaned over the refrigerated case and took a healthy sniff.

What are you doing, Kelly? asked Mr. Dell, the store manager.

What's that smell? I asked.

He bent down and took a sniff too.

Mushrooms, he said.

Do they all smell like that? I asked as I moved over to the button variety.

Like what? he said. They just came in this morning. They're fresh.

I was too busy sniffing to answer. Bill's smell was slightly saltier, a little funkier, but definitely in the same family. Mr. Dell watched me for a bit then went back to marking groceries with his price gun.

When I got home, I couldn't find Bill. He wasn't in the house, but the kitchen cupboards were open and he'd left a bunch of empty cans on the counter. I pulled my fleece tight around me and trotted off to see if he was in the shed. Not there either. It wasn't until I was heading back to the house that I saw him in our field, crouched down, barely visible in the lavender dusk. Both his hands were planted on the soil and wet clumps of grass brushed against his jeans. He was perfectly still, his head turned towards a band of dark clouds in the west.

I walked closer. His head tilted slightly as he tracked a line of birds flying across the southern sky. He still hadn't seen me. Standing there in the field, seeing my husband crouched down with his hands in the earth, a huge wave of loneliness washed over me, the kind that feels like watching a car drive away, or a long night in a hospital waiting room.

Sweetie?

He didn't hear me.

Sweetie, I said again, louder this time. What are you doing?

He gave a small start and turned towards me.

He stood up and brushed the dirt from his palms. In the distance, I saw the silver glint of the marsh, a brief flash of brilliance in the fading light. He turned to look at the line of birds as they flew towards the water, then again at me.

Just looking at the birds, Kelly, he said, and reached for my hand. I didn't want him to touch me. I wanted to flail my arms, push him in the chest, yell at him. I'd never felt that way about him before. He just smiled and kept holding out his hand until I finally took it. While we walked back to the house, I took deep breaths and kept telling myself, he hasn't done anything wrong, he hasn't done anything wrong.

Since it was cold that night, I asked Bill to get us some firewood after dinner. I was still unsettled, but at least the food had calmed me down. When he stood up, he made a quiet sound, like static or Velcro, and I could see white strands drifting from where his jeans had touched the chair. After he left, I scooted over to take a closer look. The strands were gossamer thin, floaty, pale as spider silk. I grabbed a pair of kitchen tongs and scooped them into a Tupperware container for later examination.

Bill came back in with an armload of logs, his nose buried in the wood, as I cleared our dishes from supper.

Does it smell good? I asked.

He held out his arms. I bent down and took a whiff and had to agree, the scent was amazing. He put his armload down near the woodstove, then ambled off to get more. One load turned into two, then four, then basically he emptied the whole woodshed and piled the logs in the corner of our living room. I worried about spiders for a while, but bit my tongue. He has a right to his hobbies, same as me.

I decided not to tell him about my mushroom revelation at the grocery store until I was on firmer ground, research-wise. Since he kept telling me he felt great, I decided to put my sickness theories aside and focus just on what I knew for sure. I put mushrooms, floaty white strands, Prairie City and Unity into the search engine and page after page started filling my screen. It turns out *the largest living fungus in the world* is in Malheur County, right near where he went on his trip. I kept reading and learned that humans have more genes in common with fungi than either of us do with plants. Suddenly, everything started to lock into place. When he first got back from his trip, he told me that one night they'd run around barefoot pretending to be ninjas. Maybe that's when he connected with the giant fungus, like it recognized something in him and attached.

The next day was my day off, so I decided to drive up north and finally get to the bottom of the whole situation. Once I got to Unity, I headed for the Malheur Forest Visitor Center. I figured if anyone could tell me about the giant fungus, it would be there. When I walked in, there was a sturdy lady behind a wooden counter. She wore a green uniform and her name tag said Ranger Beatrice. I wasn't sure how to approach this one, so I just launched in and asked if she knew anything about fungus and mushrooms in the area.

They're the same thing she said. Mushrooms are just fungus fruit.

See? I was learning already.

Well, I said, I hear there's a giant fungus up here.

There is, she said, waving her arms. It lives underground, it's 8,000 years old, and it's the size of sixteen Pentagons! She seemed pretty excited about it.

Is it a good fungus? I asked. I'm not totally sure what I meant by that, except for the fact that Bill is a really good man.

That depends on your perspective, she said. If you're a tree probably not since it eats trees, although just the ones that are sick or weak. But it's just doing its thing, you know? It's just living its life.

That doesn't sound quite right, I said, shaking my head. My husband would never go after someone weak. I chewed my lip while I thought. Are there other kinds of fungus around here? Like ones that are protective? I asked.

She cocked her head at me. I could tell she was interested.

Well, she said, there are so many. Her eyes drifted to the wood rafters, stayed there for a minute, then drifted back. We've identified a new fungus a few miles outside of town, but we don't know what it does yet. She leaned forward. Want to go look?

Absolutely, I said.

She grabbed her keys and strode out the door while I skittered along behind her. We took her ranger jeep, hooked a left at the reservoir, then bounced up a gravel road into the mountains. We parked at a trailhead then hiked through juniper and sage until we reached a glade at the edge of a lake. We weren't there more than a minute before a subtle shimmer pulsed through the soles of my boots. I had those suckers laced up tight and I'd put a double layer of saran wrap in them that morning. After Bill told me about running around barefoot, I figured it made sense to take precautions. Whatever the shimmer was, it was strong enough to make it through three layers. Four if you count the socks. I looked over at Beatrice, surprised.

Can you feel that? she whispered.

I nodded.

We think that's electricity.

Electricity? I whispered.

We were both whispering since it felt like a church in that glade.

Yes, electricity, she said. It's one of the ways fungi communicate.

As we walked around the glade, she told me in a low voice how fungi are everywhere, how they change as the world changes, and how life as we know it wouldn't exist without them. I ran my hands through purple asters and yellow rabbitbrush. The soft green branches of a western larch swayed in the breeze and bees swam through the burnished grass. It was the healthiest, happiest glade I'd ever seen, and I knew deep in my heart that it was the fungus helping it be that way, because that's exactly the kind of guy Bill is. While Beatrice spooned dirt into test tubes, I walked to the edge of the lake and stood where Bill must have stood all those months before. A blue heron lifted off from the northern shore, a glittering spray of water trailing from its wings. I watched it fly until I couldn't see it anymore.

Bill was sitting in our field when I got back, leaning against a fence post, looking in the direction where I had been all day. No matter what, I could see that he'd always be keeping an eye on me. Around him, a soft cloud of purple asters had started to bloom. I knew they hadn't been there the day before. I sat down next to him, our shoulders touching. The sun had just set and stars were beginning to show in the deep-blue eastern sky.

Did you know about the fungus? I asked.

Not at first, he said.

Why didn't you tell me?

His lips barely moved anymore. When he did talk, his voice was a subterranean rumble. I could hear him better if I pressed my hands to the earth.

You would have tried to stop it, sweetheart, he said.

He's right. I would have. No one else had ever loved me the way he did.

His shirt was rolled to his elbows. A spray of brown saucers, smaller than pennies, dotted his forearms and a cluster of orange fronds peeked from the neck of his sweatshirt. He told me in his new earth voice that he had reached the fruiting stage. As much as I tried to breathe and let the fear pass through me, that scared me. He gave me a gentle smile and told me not to worry, that the mushrooms were temporary, like apples on a tree or strawberries on a vine, and that they'd reflect who he is at his core; solid and patient, smelling of dirt and leaves, grounded and warm.

I asked him what comes after that and he said he didn't know.

I put my head on my knees. I could feel tears in the corners of my eyes.

Stay, I thought. Just stay.

But I knew that wasn't possible anymore. For either of us.

I pressed my forehead to his, then got up to pack my bags.

Broken Skins

Patricia Farrell

Leaning against the barn like an old shovel,
my hair twining across sticky brow, my
hands swat at those who leave
incisions and penetrations, their map of
of summer's little hurts.

The wasps gather to suckle
at the ooze of ripe apples, split
against hard ground, each fallen fruit
a result of unseen abscission,
the slow dissolution of grip.

Below the thin dermis layer,
muscles tear, ligature weakens.
It's what happens, the doctor says,
pointing to the x-ray, my bones,
damaged fruit. Ligaments as loose
as a leaf before windfall.

I'm tearing up whole plants now,
readying them for the processor.

No more selective snipping
or tender pinches. It's time for sharp
blades, scalpels, scrapers.

No salve can heal the flayed tendon
deep inside bony cuff. It's up
to metal bolts and pins
to hold us up. Salvage
what we can of our labors,
our bodies.

Where the Ground Falls

Bill Schreiber

is stones smoothed by rain
burdock's prickly orbs finding socks
as bramble scratches weep blood
and a cold steeps, burdens
breath rasping against its dry.

Grief is a hard line
a split lip, a bruised fist
harrows to flatten furrows
plant no seed but
breed stone each spring
cut bones buried in the earth.

Memory leaves us all of it.
The day's smell of browned apple peels
coffee grounds in the mulch pail
the dark within the crescent moon's whisp.
I ache for a smell I don't remember
a thing I held but fell through my fingers.

Aural

Rich Kenefic

In my dream it's morning
and grandma Mary sings to herself.
Old Italian songs, Christmas carols, Mitch
Miller on the album cover. I am thirteen,
maybe younger. She tells me I have
a good voice, returns to her cooking,
she likes roasted garlic on thin sliced
Italian bread, she gives me Augustine's
Confessions. She's at the airport
with her husband Joe, they seem
so old at this moment. It's the first time
I think of them as old. They are going
to visit my sister for the last time. I watch them
walk down the long corridor. It's hard
to bury a granddaughter. Now those days
melt into mourning. On the airplane
the engines scream their arias
into thinning air, past the threshold
of pain, I am watching the ground
fall away. I am reading from John,
something about seeing Him as He really is.
I thought I could do this. "Beloved...the Word

of God." I am walking back to my seat.
My brother places his hand in mine.
It's time to go home now.

At Jensen's beach my brother and I walk
where the sandpipers flow in search of
crustaceans slow to bury themselves. The wind
sends the sea foam tumbling, like a piper
disassembling, and there are five others
on their boards catching waves. No one
at the house of refuge where he tells me
how the waves break twenty yards
from the rocks, and how one caught the skeg
on his board and delivered him face first
into this hard place. We walk, the wind and waves
salting us down while I comb for the shell
that will tell me why I'm here, shouting again,
every time the wind takes the words away.

The Carcass of the Deer

Ty Zhang

Somewhere very near to here,
Snow slips off a tired bough.
Elsewhere,
A stag lies safely buried under snow,
Eyes closed,
A waiting summer palace for the worms.
In a place further still,
Some make music while others toil
Beyond their years,
And children chase laughter with fear.
What nonsense would it be,
In the midst of all these things,
To hold on to my bitterness?
When there is so much to be done
That even the dead have a role to play,
And I can take part.
I should remember:
It is right that the nourished gather their strength
Though the nurturers weaken and fall.
If only they could and knew enough,
They would laugh at me and what I call misery—

The toilers, the music-makers, the children, the worms,
The careworn bough,
The carcass of the deer.

The Thicket

Ahrend Torrey

> *"In a murderous time*
> *the heart breaks and breaks*
> *and lives by breaking.*
> *It is necessary to go*
> *through dark and deeper dark*
> *and not to turn."*
>
> —Stanley Kunitz

We're in the thicket: the thicket concealing stars: the thicket filled with that which can't be seen beyond us—which is right before our eyes? Keep trudging. *Or should we turn?* No, keep pushing branches from your eyes: thorns, let them drag, tear the tender membrane of your skin. A pack of coyotes howl in the frozen field beyond us— straight ahead and slightly to the right, which is possible, they could encircle us! Keep trudging. *Or should we turn?* No, keep trudging toward home—

The Tiny Library

Shaun Haurin

The offensive texts began appearing in the Tiny Library around the time of Halloween: mimeographed sheets of ink-fragrant paper stapled together in sad imitation of a bookbinding, attributed to no author, per se, merely an anonymous typed signature at the blotchy composition's end: A Concerned Citizen.

An excitable parent expressed concerns of her own when she discovered one of the blurry booklets at the bottom of the baby stroller, stashed beneath the diaper bag, along with a crumpled pack of Pall Malls, by a cagey au pair.

"Some creep is using the Tiny Library as a kind of extremist propaganda box!" she informed anyone bored or belligerent enough to listen. "Pilar told me it's not the first time. The political cartoons alone are enough to curl your hair!"

"But what if your hair's already curly?" one of us asked, our resident wiseguy. He waggled his defiantly unkempt eyebrows, shaggy as anchovies. "What else might it curl, eh?"

We stared him down. "Not to make light," he murmured.

Enough of us were alarmed by the woman's rant that eventually the authorities were notified. But the township police, who claimed to have more pressing matters on their hands—stoned skateboarders? Uncurbed dogs? Night-blind retirees running stop signs?—were reluctant to take action. The booklets were dismissively attributed to an anonymous pimply-face teen looking to catch a pretty, likeminded classmate's eye.

"Ten to one a girl's involved," said the blockheaded officer not assigned to the case. "It'll run its course, like a bad cold. Mark my words."

"Got a pen?" the wiseguy quipped.

"What?"

"A pen," he repeated. "You know, to *mark your words.*"

A week later another volume appeared, denser and blotchier than the first, as if some baffling ante had been upped.

"Is this going to be a weekly thing?" somebody wondered aloud.

"I just listened to a podcast on the Golden Age of zines," somebody else offered. "Man, they cranked those things out like holiday cookies!"

"What about the children!" cried a woman I didn't recognize. Which isn't to say she looked odd or in any way out of place. In fact, she blended in so seamlessly with the rest of us I hadn't noticed her before she spoke.

She made a good point. The Tiny Library, you see, was located at the edge of a quaint communal "play area" (neighbors preferred the term "communal" to "public," as non-residents weren't encouraged to use the facility). It was a bright, well-tended, liberally wood-chipped space overrun by nannies and their toddling, juice box-fueled charges—when it wasn't overrun by a family of irascible, loose-boweled Canadian geese.

"Kids can't even reach into the Tiny Library, let alone work that confounded latch," our resident crank helpfully pointed out.

It was true. I myself had had trouble opening the plexiglass-paneled door, on the few occasions I'd resorted to the subpar, chronically dog-eared selection afforded by the Tiny Library.

"My daughter's ten. She can reach just fine."

"Mine too."

"She's already asking the sort of questions her stepfather and I can't answer."

"Or won't answer," mumbled the crank.

"Has anybody actually read it?" someone asked. "The... proclamation, or whatever."

"Proclamation? It's a goddamn scratch pad."

"I wouldn't touch that thing with a broomstick putter!"

"Agreed," said the crank. "Read it and he wins."

"Or *she* wins," offered the wiseguy.

"Oh, please," said the woman I both did and did not recognize. "Women have better things to do than foist their half-assed dissertations on their unsuspecting neighbors."

"What about that wackadoo who wrote the SCUM Manifesto? My podcast mentioned her by name."

"Enough with the podcasts."

"People, please," said our self-appointed voice of reason. The man was a teacher by trade and a politician by nature. "We're getting off-track. Let's focus on the degenerate responsible for producing this amateurish piece of trash and see that he's brought to justice!"

"Or her."

"Yeah, right."

Someone suggested padlocking the Tiny Library to prevent the culprit from depositing his handmade magazines. But doing so would also prevent respectable citizens like ourselves from borrowing books, which, after all, was the whole point of the Tiny Library, at least in theory.

"We'll designate a key holder," suggested the born politician, who clearly had himself in mind. "Someone we trust to keep track of who borrows which books when."

"Sounds like an invasion of privacy," said the crank.

"It sure beats a *home* invasion, though."

"Huh?"

"Have you never read Orwell?" The Tiny Library, it was safe to assume, didn't stock Orwell. "Paging Big Brother…"

A week later a third volume appeared, warm as a loaf of freshly baked bread.

"And right under the children's noses!"

"Technically, the zines are *above* the children's noses," said the wiseguy.

Someone suggested affixing a surveillance camera, or at least a discouraging floodlight, to a nearby tree.

"Paid for by whom?" asked the crank.

"The township should cover it."

"Strictly speaking," said the born politician, "the township isn't affiliated with the Tiny Library."

"Then who is?"

Research conducted at the town's venerable Public Library—limestone-faced Goliath to the Tiny Library's slingshot-toting David—confirmed that its diminutive distant relation had been erected by a now-deceased private citizen some twenty years before.

"So, who's actually in charge of the Tiny Library?"

"Nobody," said the woman I no longer failed to recognize.

"Everybody," said the born politician.

"It takes a village."

"Depends on the village," huffed the crank.

"*If thy right eye offend thee, pluck it out,*" said our resident Man of God. He'd been biding his time, waiting for the most opportune moment to quote scripture.

"Oh, no!" most of us cried.

"Oh, yes."

"But the Tiny Library has been here forever," the formerly unfamiliar woman I suddenly realized I was married to pointed out. "It's an important and useful part of our lovely, enviable neighborhood, not unlike the wooden footbridge, or the golf course."

"Which golf course?"

"Twenty years isn't forever," said the crank, to whom the years, to be perfectly frank, had not been kind. "I've got ball markers older than that!"

"You've got *balls* much, much older than that," chirped the wiseguy.

"If a tree dies," the crank went on, uncharacteristically ignoring the insult, "we chop it down or tear it up by the roots, don't we?"

We agreed that we did.

"Even perfectly healthy trees are routinely taken down, if it affords us peace of mind or a better view," he continued, not unreasonably. "Are you suggesting that the Tiny Library—basically a pole with a box of used books balanced on top—is more important than a stately New England *tree?*"

He made a good point. Were we suggesting that? And if not, what exactly were we suggesting?

The day the Tiny Library was removed—uprooted, sure, like a dead or undesirable tree—I stood by and watched along with everyone else, grim-faced but not without a growing sense of vindication. After all, what choice did we have? If there was blood on our hands, it would wash off easily enough under a garden hose. (It would certainly wash off more easily than printer's ink!) No, I'm convinced we did the only sensible thing, under the circumstances.

We still don't have a clue as to the identity of the so-called Concerned Citizen. What we do know, or rather feel, is a lingering sense of having narrowly escaped some personal calamity, like a commuter who misses his usual train home and is later informed of a derailment that kills everyone onboard. For who knows what perverse or provocative notions might have taken root if we hadn't, as a community, taken swift if regrettably severe action? Who knows how unrecognizable that very community might've become, if even one among us had succumbed to the twisted wishes of the cowardly Concerned Citizen and actually read his—or her—dubious life's work?

Destructive People

Maia Brown-Jackson

Maybe there's something inside us,
inside each of us,
that might destroy us.
And for some people
it's right up close near the surface,
and either they're eaten alive
from the inside out
or they learn early on how to beat it.
But for some people it's way deep down,
and they can spend their whole life
dancing on a razor's edge with it,
never knowing if they're going to
touch
and
implode,
or explode,
or if somehow,
they can exist symbiotically,
letting it feed just enough
that it doesn't try to come out any further,
but not so much that it gets too powerful.
You know what I mean?

So what would you rather?

Rather what?

Rather have inside you?
Something that could destroy you at any second,
right up under your skin,
or way down deep?

I don't know, I say.
I don't much like to think of myself
as a destructive person, you know?

We're all destructive people, she replies.
We're all capable of destroying someone else
the second they trust us with something precious.
It's not even that we mean to;
that's just life.
So what, you never get close to anyone
because you're scared you might hurt them?

I don't really know what to say.
Yes, I'm thinking, that's exactly it.
I don't trust myself not to be selfish,
or oblivious,
or just get caught up in some
heated argument and say something
I can never take back.
And I don't think I'm so great or anything,

not that so many people would want to open up to me,
but I'm also not so great that
I should risk the chance.
Sometimes I worry I AM that destroying force,
and there's just something human left
down
deep
inside,
clawing to get out,
but it never feeds enough to get
so strong that it can break free,
and—

Woah, she says, where did you go?

I blink.
I've just been staring blankly at her, I realize.
Sorry, I say, sheepishly, I guess near the surface.

So other people could get a glimpse and know to stay away from you?

That's right.

But if it were deep down
you might never have to face it.

I wouldn't like to take that chance.

Hmm, she muses. I don't know.
I'd like it near the surface
so I could beat it, I think.

And goddamn,
isn't that just an incredible thing to say?

In Apocalypse Where Do We Gaze

Randy Bynum

I am not alive, not in playground-weld framework
of what you think, not life as up-tightly defined,

but who really gets to name-claim stuff anyway?
The Atlantic Meridional Overturning Circulation

that's who, neither wolf nor dog nor catamaran,
nor a binary either-or in sight but a tipping fall,

a woops over-hot-usury south-north-south slipping,
slowing our world to frozen and burned, low food

crop trickle in maybe 400 moons, all monsoons
lost at sea, UK farms iced, deep dive marine life

no longer to thrive, not in the same jaunty way
of what has billion years been, but then...then,

there's always Paris, and chapel and moonlight
no matter how cold, so touch my face love; begin.

My Day in the World

Jim Jas

There was a pamphlet
in the post today.
It was calling
for the attention of war.
Saying
it was my duty
to answer.

We have just
finished drawing.
My son drew
rock-like circles.
My daughter drew
our house in rainbows.
She chose rainbows,
she said,
because the three of us
are inside.

Their mother
used to get them
ready for preschool.

It's much harder in the
winter; there are
more clothes;
it just takes longer.

The subway is always full
of faces staring into
screens of misinformation.
That's why the election turned:
people can no longer crack the ice.
When everyone has a voice,
no one can be heard.

I fell in love with a colleague
two weeks after I met her.
She's much younger, and she
doesn't know.
I thought about telling her,
until I overheard that phone call.

It's amazing how the hours sink
between waking up and
going back.
Why are we drowned in meetings
about meetings until a particular
hour has arrived.

I'm still thinking about
that pamphlet.

How it announced itself
to me.

Did it know about
my family's past?
When we burned
behind fences in the 40s.
I always thought they wore
stripes so that I didn't
need to carry a uniform.

For the last meal of the day
we eat fruit salad.
The kids' favorites are grapes
and raisins.
I try to tell them that raisins
are grapes and that grapes
are raisins—
but they can't understand.

It takes time for them
to brush their teeth.
They like to switch toothbrushes
or ask for new ones.
They always start,
and I always finish.

When I read them
goodnight-stories,

we like to curl-up
in the corner of the sofa.
My son sits to my left;
my daughter sits to my right.

I can't forget the pamphlet,
but its message is starting to turn.
Where in the pain I find this,
I'm unsure,
but the letters now say:
"there's only one place
for love in this world,
and it's in you."

Today Is A Good Day! (and Other Blatant Lies)

Gabryél Grimm-Goretez

Derogatory degenerate
December marks us with death
Depressingly distressing
Distrusting
Why am I so
Disappointed
Differently arranged
Or just truly deranged?
Yet I go forth unchanged
Revelations in the shame
Do you ever miss a craze?
Nostalgia for propaganda
Grandeur, delusion, reclusive, mutually exclusive, abuse of illusion,
human ruin, there's no conclusion.

The Unhoused in the City

Cecil Morris

The city said or really shouted the difference
between sidewalk and street, like the hardness factor
and varied purposes. City admonished us
to know our places and where, without sidewalks laid,
we were not wanted, not meant to be, where our kind
was criminal and blight like dark it meant to keep
at bay. The city smiled and slapped down camping bans.
The city swept the sidewalks and scoured the parks
and kept what it wanted for itself and said as
it had said before the importance of motion
and silence and instituted fines. The city said
and said if not in words in actions look at bears
and foxes, at scavengers that wander where not
invited. See what happens, learn, evaluate
our choices, move along and keep away. It said
as clear as could be in words and deeds to seek out
some thorny wilderness of blackberry brambles
dense and dark and far from city sidewalk or street,
neither of which, it so happens, is there for us.

Female, 49, Amsterdam

Alison Boulan

The streets of the trailer park are lined with rusty pickups. Pam carefully steers around them, praying she doesn't hit one. Just as she begins to relax, a German Shepard charges at her minivan, threatening to break its chain. Gasping, she touches her crucifix. Minutes later she pulls into a driveway. The trailer is gray, and its windows are covered with plywood. A massive satellite dish hovers on top, and a blue light shines over the front door. Thanking God for protecting her, she then leaves the minivan, climbs five shaky stairs and goes inside.

A large man is sitting behind a desk covered with a yellow rotary phone, a plastic tray holding sheets of paper, and a soup can filled with pencils. He's tanned, with close-cropped gray hair, and is wearing a button-up dress shirt. Before Pam can introduce herself, the phone rings.

"Big Larry's," the man says, with a booming voice. "Leo, you goofy bastard, how's it going? Yeah, I know—I lost five hundred on that deal. I'm good. The old lady's good, too. No, she didn't take that job, because they wanted her to make doughnuts, and there's no way she's gonna make doughnuts. Listen, I gotta go—somebody just walked in. Love ya, buddy."

Pam steps forward and says, "Is this where I fill out my application?"

"Yep," the man says, leaning back in his chair, "right place. And you're in luck—we just got three openings." He grabs a pink yardstick and points at a door-sized chalkboard. "Those came in yesterday. You need to hurry though, because we got a fast turnaround."

Pam turns and reads the board:

Female, 15, Iowa City

Female, 15, Iowa City

Male, 63, Istanbul

"You're looking for a female, right?" He stands and hovers over her.

She takes a step back and nods.

"Good. We don't like mixing sexes. When you stick a woman's soul into a man's body, or a man's soul into a woman's body, it can turn into a real goat screw." He hands Pam a sheet of paper and two pencils. "Fill this out and bring me two thousand dollars. Cash. And I want all twenties. If you wanna fill it out here, you can sit over there."

Pam glances at the table, and her heart begins to thump. "Don't you have any questions for me?" she asks. "Like about my life?"

"Nope. We don't care about who, what, where and why. Just fill out the form, get the money, and we'll talk."

The red Formica table is sticky. Pam cleans it with alcohol pads and then finishes the job with a handful of tissues. The retired house-keeper is wearing her church clothes—lavender skirt, white blouse, tiny pearl earrings—and her shoulder-length, auburn hair is pulled back with barrettes. Her milky, blue eyes scan the form: it asks for her name, phone number and birthdate. And below is a list of questions. She picks up a pencil covered with teethmarks and begins answering.

"*1. Would you rather be a monkey or a kangaroo?*"

"That's easy," she mutters to herself. "Kangaroo."

"*2. Would you rather ride a bike or climb a tree?*"

"Easy again." She writes, "Ride a bike."

"3. Would you sacrifice your life to stop an asteroid from destroying the planet?"

Sucking in a breath, she says, "Stop an asteroid? This must be some kind of riddle." She laughs to herself and writes, "Yes," and then moves on.

"4. Would you be willing to die in one hour to begin your new life?"

Pam looks at the man, who's shuffling through other applications. "It's why I'm here, right?" she says, suddenly worried. Her hand shakes, when she writes, "Yes"

"6. Would you be willing to live in Afghanistan?"

"No," she whispers, laying down the pencil. "I would not be willing to live in Afghanistan." Then she remembers the Christmas no one bought her a present. And the loneliness that eats away at her like a cancer. Picking up the pencil, she writes, "Yes," and then pushes back her chair.

When she returns her application, the man studies it and says, "Okay, Pam, looks good. I'll hang onto this until you get the money, and then we'll see if you qualify for a soul-drop. Females go quick, so don't drag your feet on this. Just bring me those twenties."

"I already have the money," she says proudly. "After I saw your flyer at the laundromat, I sold my grandmother's jewelry and closed a bank account. I do have tens though—will that be a problem?"

He exhales loudly. "Sure, why not…I'll take tens. I get a good vibe from you. I'll be giving you a call within forty-eight hours, so don't leave town. And please watch your step when you go out. If somebody fell and sued Big Larry's, my wife would have a fit."

Pam turns to leave then stops. "Excuse me—do you live here?"

"Hell no," he says. "I live in the suburbs."

"Then why is your office here and not there?"

"The soul interchange runs through this place. That's why there's a satellite dish on the roof."

"Aren't you afraid somebody might break in?"

The man laughs loudly. "That'll never happen. My buddy lives next door, and he watches over the place. The guy's got swords, and you don't mess with swords."

"I have one more question—are you Big Larry?"

"Nope, that was my dad." He points to a portrait on the wall. "I'm Larry Jr., but you can call me Larry. Some of my golf buddies—" The phone rings, and he says, "Hang on."

Pam studies the picture of Big Larry, a ham-faced man, who has Larry's square jaw. She then looks around the trailer, at the fake wood paneling and corn-colored linoleum, and then spots two plastic baseball bats standing in a corner. Larry's hoarse laughter startles her, and she turns to face him.

"Leo," he says, "didn't I just talk to your crazy ass? I know, right? That happens to me all the time. Let's get—wait a sec." He waves Pam out the door. "Leo, you know I got stuff to do. *What?!* She said *what?!*"

Pam holds onto the stairway's loose railing and nearly falls. Finally safe inside her minivan, she whispers, "Thank you, God, for watching over me today. And thank you for Larry, who's helping me find a new life."

On the way home she stops to visit Pastor Edwards to say goodbye. He welcomes her into his office with a smile and is eating macaroni salad from a Tupperware container. Near his right hand, sits a fist-sized blueberry muffin, and a chipped teacup.

"What brings you in?" he asks, as Pam sits across from him. "I never see you on Tuesdays."

"I just left my girlfriend's house," she replies, "and wanted to say hello." These words fill her with guilt; she just lied to her pastor, and she'll carry this sin into another life.

"Margie Stephens is helping with the fundraiser," Pastor Edwards says, toying with a noodle. "She's a real pro with these events. We're going to have the dunk tank, too—everybody loves the dunk tank."

Pam sighs. The fundraiser is the highlight of her summer; it's when she feels love from the rest of the congregation. Everyone laughs at silly jokes, someone always gives her a hug, and children race around her legs shouting, "Pam! Pam! Pam!"

Pastor Edwards points at the muffin. "Would you like half? I'm happy to share it with you."

"Thanks for offering," she says, "but I have soup on the stove." Another lie. She's now lied to Pastor Edwards twice, all because she wants a new life.

"Okay, then," she says, standing. "It's always nice to see you."

He gives her a warm smile and says, "God's watching over you."

Taking the long way home, she passes her old high school, the library and the grocery store. Jerry works at the grocery store, the cashier who once invited her to a bowling tournament. (She declined, afraid he'd want to kiss her.) Next, she drives by the movie theater and remembers Tracy Sanders. When Pam was a girl, she and Tracy spent countless hours in the front row, eating popcorn and laughing at nothing. The memory fills her with sadness, and she asks herself, "Am I ready to leave this all behind?"

Back at home, she takes off her shoes and digs her toes into a pair of fuzzy slippers. Sunlight fills the living room, lifting her spirits, and she goes to the kitchen for pretzel sticks and ginger ale. Carrying her snacks to the sofa, she stops to study the pictures across the room: parents, grandparents, great-great grandparents, aunts, uncles and cousins. Peanut and Jelly Bean, her two dead cats, are there too, both gazing at her with adoring eyes.

Pam drapes a comforter across her lap, switches on the TV and rewatches an old episode of *The Oprah Winfrey Show*. She's saved this episode, because Hillary Clinton is the guest, and she loves Hillary as much as she loves Oprah. After sipping her ginger ale, she wonders if the girls in Iowa City watch *Oprah*; she'll have to ask Larry this; she'd really like to know. A gutter commercial takes over the TV, and she studies a pretzel stick, telling herself she'll buy them in Iowa City, too. When the commercial ends, Pam looks up, just as Oprah swallows Hillary with a hug.

The phone rings, and she says, "Hello?"

A deep voice replies, "Pam, how's it goin'?"

"Hi, Larry. I'm watching *Oprah*."

"*Oprah?* You're kidding me…whatever floats your boat. Pam, you're good to go. I got you locked in with a fifteen-year-old. You need to attend a class, and you're scheduled for tomorrow morning. It lasts thirty, forty minutes, and I'll have sloppy joes, tater tots, coffee and beer. Smoking's okay, but no weed."

"Larry," she says, after licking her lips, "can I have time to think about it?"

"No can do, Pam. I like you, but we gotta strike while the iron's hot. If we wait too long, somebody might snatch her up. Class starts at eleven and be careful coming into the trailer park. There was a shooting last night, some fight over a motorcycle. Police caught the guy, but folks are still jumpy. Nobody likes gunfire. Nobody."

While lying in bed that night, Pam prays before falling asleep. "God," she says, "thank you for the joy you're bringing into my life. Give me the strength to overcome the trials I'll be facing and help me share your love and joy." She then falls asleep and dreams about Larry and Pastor Edwards falling into a dunk tank.

Pam approaches Larry's trailer the next day and finds an old car in the driveway. She carefully climbs the stairs, walks inside, and is greeted by the smell of fried potatoes and cooked hamburger.

Larry leaves the kitchen holding a spatula. "Pam," he says affectionately, "nice to see you again. Take a seat and say hello to Monique."

The two women avoid eye contact, and Pam drops into a lawn chair across the room. Larry returns with Styrofoam plates; each holds an oozing sloppy joe, six tater tots and a plastic fork. Handing them to the women, he says, "Careful now—it's hot."

Pam glances at Monique, an overweight Black woman, with round cheeks speckled with moles. Her purple polyester dress hugs her waist, and she smells of mouthwash and patchouli oil. Pam's eyes then drop to the plate on her knees. Orangey grease is leaking through the bun, and she moves the soppy mess aside, before stabbing a tater tot and forcing it into her mouth.

"Ladies," Larry says, "let's get to it. Any questions before we get started?"

Pam raises her hand. "Why are the girls from the same city?"

"Good question, Pam—they're twins. We rarely get twins, and I think the last time was those men from the Congo. Anything else?"

Monique says, "I have a question—what's going to happen to them? Will they be okay?"

"No idea," Larry replies. That information never comes down the pipeline."

Pam stands. "I'm worried about those girls. Pastor Edwards wouldn't want me to cause another person's suffering, and if my soul-drop might hurt someone, I'd want to know."

Larry scratches his head. "Pastor Edwards? Who's that? Listen, we know sex, age and city. That's it. Now if this suffering bothers you two, just hit the door, because there's people behind you." They women stay silent, and he says, "Okay then. Monique, what's your story?"

"Well," she says quietly, "everybody left me. My husband moved back to Atlanta, and my kids are all grown. I stopped going to church when our minister left, and my best friend, Rhonda, died of that CO-VID. But I felt alone as a girl, too. It was like something was missing, something real deep, something—"

"Monique," Larry says, "let me stop you there. Would you two like dessert? My wife made some raisin tarts, and I can throw on a pot of coffee."

"Yes," Pam says, glad for a change in mood. "I think we'd love some raisin tarts."

Larry returns with two tarts and napkins. "Get ready," he says, beaming. "You're in for a real treat."

The women take small bites and then nod in agreement.

"*See*," he says, "they should be selling those at Walmart. Let me get your coffee, and I'll grab another beer."

He returns, holding Styrofoam cups filled with steaming coffee. Carefully placing one in each woman's hand, he says, "Let me know if it's too hot, and I can get you an ice cube."

Back at his desk, Larry opens his beer. "Pam," he says, "let's hear from you."

"I've been lonely my whole life," she responds, after wiping the corner of her mouth. "And I'm not married either. In fact, I've never even been with a man—I hope that's not too personal."

"We're all friends here," Larry says, hopping onto the desk. "I got troubles, too. I was a real hell-raiser in my twenties, but that's another story. Go ahead, Pam. Sorry for interrupting."

"Larry, it feels like I'm floating through life, like I have a hole in my heart and don't know how to fill it."

"That's so sad," Monique says, touching Pam's elbow. "And I think you spoke for me. My marriage was a disappointment from day one. He worked the nightshift, and I had to sleep alone in our big bed. And then I'd cook him breakfast, while he watched TV. He missed my birthday one year, and I—"

Larry interrupts her. "Your husband sounds like a real jackass, but we need to get going. Ladies, here's the drill. When these two girls are ready to pass on, we drop you in. You get their bodies, but you're giving them new souls. It'll give you a chance to steer their lives in a new direction. Pam, you have your hand up."

"What happens to their souls? Do they go into somebody else's body? And I want to ask about *Oprah*—do the girls watch *Oprah?*"

"*Oprah?* Pam you need to let go of *Oprah*. This is serious. Now to get back to your first question, my dad said their souls land in some in-between place, sorta like a soul truck stop. Monique, you're next. Whatcha got."

"If the girls are getting ready to pass on, they're obviously going through something bad. Could we drop in when they're in the hospital? This part confuses me."

"There's a million ways to pass on, some good, some not so good, but we're not privy to that information. Let's get to the meat of this. Pam, one more question."

"Larry, what happens to our bodies during the drop-in?"

"If I tell you that, you'll stop being my friend, and I'd hate for that to happen. So, you two are going to be sisters. We don't know who's getting dropped in first but be ready. No booze, don't ride motorcycles, and don't use power tools. And *please* don't have sex. You have no idea what a mess that is."

The phone rings, and Larry reaches behind him. "*Leo*," he says, "I told you I was doing a class today. No, I don't care who's gonna be there. If he can't make it, get somebody else. *Marty*? No way...I hate that guy. Let me call you later."

Larry finishes his beer and belches. "Sorry about that. Me and Leo go way back. He's a pain sometimes, but he's good people. Where was I? Oh, the drop-in. So, when it's time, you two are going to have a nightmare that lasts eighteen minutes. It gives us a chance to turn you off for the delivery. Past nightmares were about falling out of a plane, getting attacked by bats, and stabbing someone in a knife fight."

Both women are staring at the floor, and Larry says, "Let's take a break. You guys look like you're falling asleep. Get some fresh air, and then we'll finish up. And watch those stairs. As soon as I get the money, I'm gonna buy something new. Something real sturdy."

Navigating the swaying stairway, they climb into the minivan. Pam wiggles into her seat, caresses the steering wheel and says, "Are you ready for your new life?!"

Monique's face lights up. "Yes, indeed. I didn't sleep a wink last night. It feels like my birthday and Christmas rolled into one."

"I know, right? I've never even been to Iowa City. What do you think it's like?"

"Well, they grow corn in Iowa, so the girls probably live on a farm."

"Ooh, I'd love to live on a farm. Maybe our family will have a dog, one of those farm dogs that's always happy to see you. I've always wanted a dog, maybe a Labradoodle. Those seem like nice dogs."

"I'm partial to Schnauzers. My aunt had a Schnauzer named Harvey. Couldn't ask for a better dog."

Pam turns and says, "You know what dog I don't like? Chihuahuas. You couldn't give me a Chihuahua."

"I hear that—no Chihuahuas for me either. I'd rather a goldfish than a Chihuahua. You know," she then says, facing her new friend, "I'm going to like having you as a sister."

"Stop it," Pam says, covering her face. "You're going to make me cry."

Larry suddenly appears and pounds on Monique's window. "Break's over," he shouts. "Back to work."

The two women, now renewed, climb out and scale the rickety stairs. Back inside, they fall into their chairs and then look at each other and smile.

Larry grabs the yardstick, taps the floor and says, "So you guys are going to be teenagers again. Don't be surprised if you're now playing soccer every day and doing ballet."

Pam grabs Monique hand and says, "This is so exciting!"

"You'll wanna eat well in the next few days," Larry goes on to say, "things like bananas and celery sticks. Some folks like saltines, but I was never a fan of saltines. One guy ate tacos, and boy was that a mistake. Lettuce is good too, but—"

The phone rings, and Larry groans. Grabbing the receiver, he yells, "*Leo*, what is it this time?" Emotion drains from his face, and he stops talking. Then, speaking quietly, he says, "Hi, Mr. Moretti. Yes, sir, I can talk. What's that? Really? I understand, sir—there's no need to apologize. Yes, sir, I'll get on that right away. Thank you, sir. You have a magnificent day, too."

Larry turns to the women and says, "Here we go again." He then walks over to the board, erases the first *Female, 15, Iowa City* and grabs a piece of chalk. Pam and Monique watch, with their mouths hanging open, as he writes:

Female, 49, Amsterdam

Walking to the refrigerator, he says, "Anybody want grape juice? I keep some in the fridge for when we wrap things up…it's a nice way to celebrate."

Pam's voice quivers when she replies, "No, thank you, Larry. We're fine."

He returns with a beer, takes a long drink, and then says, "Okay, here's the deal. Mr. Moretti said somebody grabbed one of the girls. It was those guys over at Southside Soul Brokers. I hate those people—they're nothing but liars and thieves. Monique, you dropped your money off first, so you're going to Iowa City. Pam, you're going to Amsterdam. Now transatlantic drop-ins take longer, so your nightmare might last forty-five, fifty minutes, and I hope that's not a problem. Ladies, I'm real sorry, but I don't have time for questions. I got another class coming in and need to get more coffee. It was nice working with you two—I really enjoyed it. And please watch those stairs when you go out. If one of you fell, I'd never forgive myself."

Dreamer

—after an untitled pen-and-ink drawing by Kunisada

Susanna Lang

She fell asleep, head pillowed
on her book. Haven't you ever
woken past midnight,

lights burning, unsure
if the images filling your mind
are from the page left open

or a chapter added in your dream?
I've been dreaming of bears
and mountains, my fat novel

still in my lap, bookmark
fallen from my place.
Kunisada's dreamer

hasn't even loosened her hair
from its pins, while overhead
a bristling ogre threatens

her lover with a sword almost
too long to lift. She sees herself
(hair still up in pins) crouching

behind the young man's back,
hand over her eyes. Meanwhile
her cat places one tentative paw

on her arm, stares into her sleeping
face—or is that my cat, urging me
to turn over, move my book,

let her curl into my side?

As Water Flows over Rock

Daniel Thomas Moran

Today, there was
a raindrop fell
from a swell of cloud,
onto the brow of
a rocky hill, and
tumbled into a rill,
that ran through
the leaning grass.

Because of this river,
nothing is ever still,
the silence of distance
is whispered away
by a wight's lullaby.

On its surface,
the brushstrokes of
an impressionist,
his palette of black
and cadmium white.

Its travels are unceasing,
under weary August sun,
or star spilt winter nights.
Monthly, the full moon,
lights upon a dance of
the ancient spirits.

It is the traveler, who
never stops to board,
who drinks of itself and
never from thirst,
a clockless watchman,
counting ages through
unimagined places.

It is ever on, to where
its burnished waters
become waves and tides,
To wear and wash the shores
of places we will never see.

Watching Anoushka Shankar and Patricia Kopatchinskaja Play "Raga Piloo" on YouTube after Scrolling through Climate Change and War News All Morning

Christien Gholson

How it all fell away, how
the raga's slow weave of
shadow and light began to
organize the chaos, reveal
those things that continually
move unseen inside me: a
cabbage moth quick-beating
pale-yellow wings above a
kale leaf, lung-bridge to heart,
heart-bridge to intestines and
spine; a raven feather falling
from a clear blue sky, tumbling
vane over quill, into a clear
blue lake; mist from rain-
damp pines and all the wander-
ing dreams of *Laetiporus* mush-
rooms clinging to dead bark;
listen, listen, the sitar and violin
strings are the root threads

that connect everything above
to everything beneath; look,
look, a child is humming,
mimicking a fuzzy horned
bumblebee while foraging
for pollen on fireweed inside
me; see, see, the first Japanese
maple leaves sail out over
the balcony inside me; leaving
me without a *without*, with
no *way out*, as the raga ends,
the last note a water bead hung
from the tip of a lavender leaf,
after the rain, after the rain,
trembling, full of potential
energy, ready to launch, from
sky to leaf to earth...

Unnaturally Hot

Robin Herzog

I.

When the summer is sizzling and the asphalt is good for frying eggs upon and the shining cobblestones of Brooklyn become suns of their own, then people change on an atomic level too. Some folks flee the heat, locked away in murky apartments, much like mushrooms—waiting, hiding, hoping for a drop of rain. Their ceiling fans whir twenty-four hours a day. They come out at night, if ever, and you might catch a glimpse of their faces if you treat them to a Chelada in a thick-walled bar. Or if they rush past you in a bodega selling dark rum and cubed ice. Others turn into devils in the heat. Absolutely everything is fought over or complained about. Insults are hurled towards the hotdog man down the street who has increased the price of the kielbasa, and the turnstile gets the evil eye for having lost its shine. These people are easily spotted getting into arguments over cab fares where they spit their anger and grow horns. Yes, these and many more types of folks change because of the heat. But the category of true interest is another one. It's a slim one and yet, its people are a mosaic since some shop at Cartier and others chew potatoes seven days a week. But however rich or poor, very few of them obsess over fortune and glory. They wake up in the sweltering heat like the rest of us, but instead of trickling sweat, dentist's appointments, rumors of downsizing and traffic for miles, they see cumulus clouds shaped like Pancho Villa above Queens and carpenter ants building chapels on Sixty-Sixth and Ninety-First Street. While yesterday, under the iron sky, they were a bit more like you and I, possibly lacking in confidence and spontaneity, they have become mavericks and more of their true selves in the lava heat. The jaw is set right, the knuckles are cracked, the gaze is daring, the lungs are filled and the soul is awake. How does it work? It doesn't really matter, but know that their curiosity is for adventure's sake, riches are not closest to heart. That makes all the difference. The way it was supposed to be long ago and the way it's supposed to be today, even though many have forgotten it.

Thus begins our story, in a New York City that even puts sub-zero freezers to the test. Our young man of the hour is Michael Mitchell—he has a curious mind and is quick to laugh. And though he does not know it yet, in the future he will be a generous man among greedier fellows and a humble man amid cut-glass elbows. A man who does not deceive to get ahead, but who takes pride in the truth and demands it from his peers. He will be a man who believes in action and who is not afraid to lose. He will be a kind man, but those who intend to exploit him will be made sorry because he will be a man with a quick wit and a boxers' right hook. And the one who talks less of him will miss his friendship since he will be a droll man and an interesting man to whom interesting events unfold. However, most of that has yet to be. Now he is only twenty-one years old and the sort of son of Brooklyn who has just begun sensing ventures around corners. But it should be known that Michael Mitchell was born Mijailo Milosevic after his late grandfather who was very much like him when it came to said qualities. He lived a full life. He crossed the Atlantic on a steamer to get to America in what now seems like another age. And years before that, in old Mijailo's day, which is to say when *old* Mijailo was *young* Mijailo, he set off from his small village, which now belongs to Croatia, to sail for a trading company headed for African nations he'd only heard of. These were in the years of coal and steel. And how could Mijailo say no? He wished to see the bushmen and the Tuaregs of the desert, he wished to see the lions. Most of all he wanted to see that which he could not imagine. When Mijailo told of his new career to his parents, who were farmers and had only seen the sea from a distance, they sighed and gave each other a look. One which had been saved between them for twenty years. They had never told Mijailo that he had been born under a red-hot sun on a day that lasted twice that of a normal day. And that the wise man of the village had professed to them that Mijailo would go to sea, never to come home to them again. The wise man had also given away that he would face many perils. Though his greatest foe would not be lurking in worlds afar.

"But you let him go when the time comes. It's a risk, but you must take it."

And let him go they did, but with tears in their eyes. On seeing his parents' sorrowful faces at the moment of departure, Mijailo gave them his old red scarf. They kept it on the kitchen table and smelled it whenever they missed him. Which was often. Seven days later Mijailo stood on the stern of the Mirjana, his new home. He was twenty years old in between two world wars, looking for purple horizons and that which is unseen but so desirable. It is something different to each and every one, and a life not permitted to pursue it, is not a life lived.

II.

Mijailo traversed the Mediterranean getting sunburned and learning the mysteries of the sea from the old, tattooed sailors. When he looked back on the Rock of Gibraltar, he was not the same boy who had left his village. He was on his way to becoming a mariner. And while the ship was named Mirjana, a modest name, its owner was English and so was the flag streaming in the wind. The English were the power in the waters and that emitted a sense of pride in him. The Mirjana laid port in The Gambia and Sierra Leoné to do business and Mijailo's jaw dropped from what he saw. But then came the Gold Coast. A name and a place that would etch a mark in his heart and follow him around for a very long time. All his life. Because there, in the mesmerizing city of Accra, he secretly fell in love with a woman of the Ashanti tribe in the tall grass on a hot day that seemed unnaturally long. Her name was Asaaseasa and it was as if the gods wanted for them to have all the time that they could have. When they met, Mijailo looked into her eyes until he was complete. And even though their love was short-lived, merely weeks old, it was true. And he owed it to himself to feel good about it. But when it was revealed among Asaaseasa's family that she had relations with a European, a white man, their love was doomed. And so was he. The love he felt for her, did, in the end, cost him almost everything. But had he not dared to go to Asaaseasa in the first place, his regret would absolutely have cost him everything. At long last they had to say farewell in the pouring rain under a barrage of threats. She lived on without him, in sorrow, and he without her. They both survived, but they never did see each other again.

Afterwards Mijailo lived many adventures in Africa and Asia and saw the purple horizons that he had once dreamed of. Whole seasons came and went. And in time his heart became lighter while his hands became strong and tough as rope. When the sun and the wind had turned Mijailos's face permanently salty and stone-like, he felt like a real sailor, and it was around then that he decided to go see his mother and father again. He smiled as he guessed that they might have trouble picking him out of a crowd. When Mijailo arrived in Croatia, however, it turned out that he was the one who struggled to familiarize himself. The countryside that had seemed so vast resembled a paddock. But time had not stood still. When Mijailo walked up the last couple of hills, he saw that the wooden village he had left had turned into a village of stone and electric lights shone as well. But no one was home when he got there. Mijailo looked around—the precious garden was unkempt, and the grass had grown tall. When the neighbors appeared, Mijailo saw that their faces were dark. In the end he found his parents' graves with tears in his eyes and buried a red scarf between the headstones on that hot day that seemed to go on forever. Thus the wise man of the village had been right about what would happen if Mijailo left the village. And so, seeing no future in his country, Mijailo looked west, to the land which was said to be promised.

III.

This has been only a nibble of the big bite which constitutes the rich, bending and colorful life of *old* Mijailo Milosevic, the sailor. But the story does not end there, no. Because *young* Mijailo Milosevic, ergo, Michael Mitchell of Brooklyn, is, as we've said, of about the same stuff as his grandfather, even though he doesn't know it. His parents can sense it, however, and although they are glad for it, they worry too. They worry that he is going to find out about it too soon for his own good. That is why they brought him books, board games and puzzles all his childhood instead of cheering him on to play outside, where the world lay. The approach worked quite well, it must be said. But all it takes for an adventure to begin, is that a person, just for a second, hears the whisper in the wind.

And so, on a scorching hot summer's day that felt unnaturally hot, Michael Mitchell walked into a bar. It was an old watering hole named Fire Station and he entered it thirsty with his two pals. At twenty-one years of age the bar scene enticed the three friends greatly, they weren't broad shouldered men who had sailed the seas and wrestled the world. They were much closer to being boys. But they weren't too young to have dreams. And since Fire Station was a cocktail bar pouring classics in a red wine-looking room with lots of Santos Mahogany and lighting like a Jerusalem sunset, it felt like a place where dreams could come true. While the others went hunting for a table, Michael took a look around. The inside was ripe with heavy fragrances and quick silhouettes. Everything was a dark blur except for a statue next to a silver door in the back. *No, not a statue,* he thought. Michael squinted; *it's a person.* He walked towards the statueesque person and the shiny door. The individual turned out to be a black-haired girl with a lit cigarette that made Michael wish he was the cigarette. He wanted to say something clever to her, but when he reached down there was nothing there, so he went for the intricately ornamented door. He had to open it for the same reason that man must go to the moon or whistle tunes while on a stroll. But Michael never got the chance to turn the handle.

"Hey, Green Shirt Guy!" Came the young woman's voice at him.

"Oh, hi."

"You want to see what's inside?"

"Umm, yeah, what is it, the men's room?"

But he already knew it wasn't the men's room.

"Men's room's back where you came from."

"So what is it?"

"What should I call you except Green Shirt Guy?"

"Michael."

However, in his mind he always answered Mijailo.

"Michael, I have a question for you."

"Yeah? Shoot."

"Do you believe?"

He couldn't explain it, but somehow he knew what she meant.

"In what?" Michael said.

"I mean do you actually believe?"

He believed. He had for some time. Though he never told anybody.

"Believe in what?"

"That your whole life can change after one taste of something... *Strange*."

"I once saw a magician put a cigarette through a silver dollar, but I didn't believe it and it didn't change anything."

"I'm not talking about street artists or dunking from the three-point line." The woman rolled her eyes. "I mean treasures beyond price. I mean saving a life. Miracles."

"I guess I do believe in some things."

"Such as?"

Gravity, falling for someone, he thought.

"Love," he said.

"Not bad, *Mike Who Believes in Love*. Because the *true* seekers don't search for gold."

"What do they want?"

"Oh you. Don't you know?" She leaned in. "Illumination."

Michael was falling for the girl.

"Alright, but really, who are you? You sound like a wizard or something."

He wanted to listen to her forever.

"I work here."

"Right. So, can I open the door?"

"If you're ready, Michael. If you must. If it's what you want to do. Because if you go in there you'll change."

Her eyes were deep and warm, but the warning in her voice overshadowed her look.

"What?"

"You'll change."

"How?"

"You'll see."

Michael looked at her and hesitated. But in the end, he gripped the door handle and turned it. And although the next moment only lasted for a blink of an eye, it was when all of Michael's dreams and wishes rose through his heart, and so did his demons. There was lightning and fire inside of him. Although it wasn't a battle, but his untold truths. And then it vanished. All of it. Because Michael had opened the door and behind it was a six-by-six foot supply closet with brooms, mops, stacks of toilet paper, detergent, soap and dish cloths. Nothing else. Nothing riveting. Nothing *strange*. But the girl who looked at Michael did so differently than before. She sensed a burst cocoon at his feet and saw someone whose posture and countenance had changed somehow. That was why she smiled. And it was true. Michael had changed somehow; he felt it too. Opening the door had been his moment, but he couldn't put it into words, so when Michael turned around from the supply closet and faced the girl, he didn't say anything. He didn't know what to say. She didn't say anything either, but she didn't have to. Her eyes and one-tenth-of-an-inch smile burned a mark in Michael's brain. So, he walked away to the bar to get a beer and collect his thoughts before returning to his friends. But just as he took the first sip, four fellows came through the entrance. The first three went for a table but the fourth one stood looking around the room. He eventually noticed the silver door. First he stared at it, then he went for it, he even brushed past Michael on his way there. But just as he was about to open it, the girl with the cigarette stepped forward.

"Sorry, bud, supply closet. Personnel only."

Michael looked on in amazement as the young man turned around and walked away. *Now why the hell didn't she say that to me? Why'd she work me over?* Michael wondered. But the thoughts vanished as the black-haired girl locked her eyes with him and flashed a wink that hit him with the force of Victoria Falls. Then she cleared a gang of glasses off a few tables and brought them to the kitchen. She was, when all came around, a bar worker, not a wizard. Michael downed his pint and looked at the kitchen door for her to reappear, but in vain. The girl never came back out. He never saw her again. So, Michael walked over to his friends, he didn't stay long, however. In fact, he left the bar minutes later. Michael couldn't sit still, he had to get going. He stood up, paced off and opened the door—a whirlwind and a setting sun before him. Across the street—a gentleman in a sports car hollering at him. In the alley to his right—a sinister-looking fellow flashing a wristwatch under his coat. To Michael's left—a pair of abandoned ladies' sunglasses and the lingering trace of cherry and musk.

New York and everything in it was waiting for him, holding its breath. It had been for a long time. There were cumulus clouds shaped like Pancho Villa above Queens and there were ants building chapels on Sixty-Sixth and Ninety-First Street. They had been waiting for him too. He had to go, he had to run. *Why was that, was he alright? You* might wonder. Yes, Michael was quite alright, he was more than alright. He had just been dubbed an adventurer in its truest form, like his grandfather before him. And assuming you are a believer, you best trust that *old* Mijailo, the sailor, was up there, somehow, somewhere, smiling, as his boy picked up the sunglasses, took to his left and ran off to find purple horizons and that which is unseen but so desirable. It is something different to each and every one of us, and a life not permitted to pursue it, is not a life lived.

Kinosake

Sam Spring

With the soft rains
That came, the land
Kept its promise of green—
Green along the calm
River passing gently through
The center of town,
In the willows silently
Weeping on its banks,
Green in the ancient hills
Grown up on all sides
That have seen countless
sunrise and moonshower,
Green even under the
Sidewalk's grate
Where the early day's
Hazy drizzle slid down upon
Proud, little leafed plants.
Green still found a way.
And now, the rain
Picks up into a downpour

—drumming a new,
Faster heartbeat on
The tin roof.
This early morning,
Like so many thousands before it,
Is the furthest we've ever been.

Love Poem

Joanne Esser

We've walked
so long side
by side, it's mostly

habit now, ease
like how clouds
slip across

clear June skies.
Sometimes I notice
purely by accident

how our steps
fall in synch
crunching the sandy

trail in a rhythm
unplanned yet perfectly
steady. How

does that happen
so quickly? Only
yesterday, it seems,

we ventured out
on our first hike, heavy
packs weighting

our shoulders, aware
of every word,
watching for self-

conscious signs
of how our fledgling
partnership might work.

Once when I tripped
hard on steep gravel,
you looked scared,

handed me a band-aid
from my first aid kit
for the blood.

Now we both stumble
regularly but don't
fall flat, few skinned knees.

We carry lighter
packs, tramp paths
less steep. We wait

for each other,
no need to impress,
no need to hurry.

The trail always
leads us
back around again.

The Lovers in Autumn

Daniel Thomas Moran

The reddened eye
of Autumn has opened,
on the island in our river.

Morning reveals in darkness.

The air is grown heavy
with the woeful weight
of a bowing summer.

We are no longer young.

We reflect on flowers,
and the dimming
damp light of August.
The September sun
is sharp and slung low in
the dwindling afternoon.

Soon the skeletons
of trees will come to dance,

The forest floor will prepare
a bed for the reclining snow.

And we, with love by our side,
with the kindling box filled, are
composed for the long nights.

The wool and flannel days
are upon us.

At the End, Song

Joanne Esser

I hope that's how it will be at the end
when souls gather to ride, crammed together

in a transparent mystical subway car, uncertain
of how they arrived, became part of this crowd,

or where they are headed. Strangers at first,
they'll begin to seem familiar, as if

they recognize each other from somewhere
long ago. Then one will start, an old soul

full of spirit and strength, to hum a low note.
Solo, his melody bold and slow. Gradually

it will expand, and one by one, each soul
will join, adding tones, some harmony, and

the song will grow, will lift, will fill
the train, a chorus swelling to the ceiling,

through open windows and beyond—
a choir of voices resonating back and forth,

among, between, and through, vibrating
joy without words. No one's voice, but

one voice
that rises and echoes and lasts.

A Blessing for the Threshold

Christine Marie

May your eyes be open and clear
so that you can see the star guiding you to
the birthplace of Mystery.

May you know the Love that is always
seeking to find you, to take root and to bloom in you,
to dwell in the tender ground of your being.

May you cross the threshold of this time
with grace and courage, knowing the power
of your mind to heal and forgive.

May prayer shelter you
from doubt, fear and fragility,
and light the path before you.

May your curiosity lead you forward,
may you be generous with the treasures of your heart,
and may your joy be full to overflowing.

Contributors

Phillip Barron is the author of two books of poetry, *What Comes from a Thing* (Fourteen Hills, 2015) and *Bright Leaf* (Horse and Buggy, 2022). He teaches poetry and philosophy at Lewis & Clark College.

John Blair has published seven books, including *Playful Song Called Beautiful* (University of Iowa Press, 2016) and last year's *The Shape of Things to Come—Poems* (Gival, 2023), as well as poems with various magazines, including *Poetry*, *The Sewanee Review*, *The Georgia Review*, *The Colorado Review*, and *New Letters*.

Michelle Boland's poems have appeared in *Bellevue Literary Review*, *Solstice Literary Magazine*, *Calyx—A Journal of Art and Literature by Women*, *Cold Mountain Review*, and *Lily Poetry Review*, among others. Her work has also been awarded runner-up in *Blue Earth Review's* Dog Daze Poetry Contest. She recently completed her first full-length poetry collection, *Burnflower*.

Alison Boulan is a photographer and writer. She lives in Michigan and does not love the state's long winter, but she does love its springtime and bees. Her work has appeared in *Lucid Stone*, *WordWrights*, *Carriage House Review*, *Natural Bridge*, *Jerseyworks*, *Pindeldyboz*, *The Dogwood Journal*, *The MacGuffin*, *Oyster Boy Review*, and *Cool Beans Lit*.

After the incredibly practical literature degree from the University of Chicago, award-winning, pushcart-nominated **Maia Brown-Jackson** then braved the myriad esoteric jobs that inevitably followed, ultimately straying to Iraq to volunteer with survivors of ISIS genocide. Inspired with a new focus, she caffeinated herself through a graduate degree in terrorism and human rights and now investigates fraud, waste, and abuse of humanitarian aid in Taliban-controlled Afghanistan. Also, she writes.

Randy Bynum's work appears in *The Good Life Review* (2024 Honeybee Prize Winner for Poetry), *Cirque* (2023 contest winner), *Arboreal Literary Magazine*, *Metonym Journal*, *Atticus Review*, *New Plains Review*, *Cathexis Northwest Press*, *Santa Clara Review*, and others. His mother was 1/2 Native American/Cherokee who hid it until late in life. His collections seeking publication include *Tulips Talking Behind My Back* and a four-volume set entitled *Dragons Who Type: Poems of Whimsy and Wishes*. He's an award-winning playwright, ("The Convert," Kennedy Center/ACTF, Region IX), and lives in Oregon with wife Dani and rescue dog Coop of the Dump.

Eric Oman Callahan is a writer from Portland, Oregon, who explores themes of family, grief, and place through fabulist stories.

Nick Conrad's poems continue to appear in a number of national and international journals. His first book, *Lake Erie Blues* (Urban Farmhouse), appeared in 2020. His podcast for *All Write in Sin City* aired in 2021.

Carina Cooper is an artist and writer who lives in Milwaukie, Oregon, with her husband and their two cats. She is a non-traditional student earning her associates degree at Clackamas Community College. She enjoys drawing, painting with watercolors and acrylics, writing fiction, and spending time with her family.

John Cullen graduated from SUNY Geneseo and worked in the entertainment business booking rock bands, a clown troupe, and an R-rated magician. Recently he has had work published in *American Journal of Poetry*, *The MacGuffin*, *Harpur Palate*, *North Dakota Quarterly*, *Cleaver*, *Pembroke Magazine*, and *New York Quarterly*. His most recent chapbook, *The Observation of Basic Matter*, will be published in 2024 by Bass Clef Books.

Dean Engle is a writer and community college instructor from the San Francisco Bay Area. He has been published in *On the Run*, *Santa Ana River Review*, *Great Lakes Review*, *The Town*, *The Ana*, *Dunes Review*, and previously in *The Clackamas Literary Review*. In his spare time he enjoys making soup and forgetting to water his beloved fern.

Joanne Esser is the author of the poetry collection *Humming At The Dinner Table,* the chapbook *I Have Always Wanted Lightning,* and most recently, *All We Can Do Is Name Them* (Fernwood Press, October 2024). Her poems appear in *Dunes Review*, *Orca*, *Wisconsin Review,* and *Third Wednesday*, among other journals. She earned an MFA from Hamline University and has been a teacher of young children for over forty years. She lives with her husband in Eagan, Minnesota.

Patricia Farrell lives in rural western Oregon. Formerly a biologist and landscape architect, she completed the Certificate of Creative Writing program from Linfield University in 2021. In 2023 she won first place in the New Poets category of the Oregon Poetry Association contest. Her poems have been published in *Paper Gardens*, *Camas Literary Journal*, *Verseweavers*, *The Thieving Magpie*, *Wild Roof Journal*, *Glassworks*, and *Stone Poetry Quarterly*. When not writing she enjoys gardening, exploring the Pacific Northwest, and admiring trees. She writes to capture memories, mental meanderings, and the wonders and despairs of living in this beautiful world.

Cathy Socarras Ferrell is a poet, writer, and educator of Cuban-French-Irish heritage. The granddaughter of immigrants, she finds inspiration in family story-telling, walking (anywhere), and the sandhill cranes in her yard. Cathy enjoys playing with form, space, and the sounds of language. Her work can be found at *Dandelion Scribes*, *Making Waves*, *Santa Clara Review*, *Novus Literary Arts Journal*, *Compulsive Reader*, and other literary journals, as well as the scholarly collection, *Shakespeare and Latinidad*, edited by Trevor Boffone and Carla Della Gotta. She is an alumna of *Tupelo Press'* 30/30 Project, October 2022, 2023, and 2024 cohorts.

Christien Gholson is the author of several books of poetry, including *The Next World* (Shanti Arts), *Absence: Presence* (Shanti Arts), and *All the Beautiful Dead* (Bitter Oleander); along with a novel, *A Fish Trapped Inside the Wind* (Parthian Books). He is the recipient of a Pushcart Prize, with work appearing in *Ecotone*, *Permafrost*, *Flyway*, *Banyan Review*, *The Shore*, *Hotel Amerika*, *Tiger Moth Review*, and *The Sun*, among other journals. He lives in Oregon and works as a somatic-oriented mental health therapist at a clinic collective.

Gabryél Grimm-Goretez is a 22 year-old, Portland, Oregon, based author, artist, and musician. Formerly trained in poetry, Gabryél has won just about every writing accolade her high school had. Inspired by gothic classics, Gabryél also enjoys blending the raw energy of the post-punk world into her projects. Her works reflect on experiences of growing up queer and mixed-racial, with a religious upbringing, while exploring themes of identity and cultural intersections. Her debut novel, *Holy Water Hurts: A Vampire's Guide To Vampire Hunting* (coming summer 2025), which was written when the author was still in high school, helps to solidify her as an up-and-comer to watch.

Colleen S. Harris is a three-time Pushcart Prize nominee whose collections include *The Light Becomes Us* (Main Street Rag, forthcoming), *Babylon Songs* (First Bite Press, forthcoming), *These Terrible Sacraments* (Bellowing Ark, 2010; Doubleback, 2019), *The Kentucky Vein* (Punkin House, 2011), and *God in My Throat: The Lilith Poems* (Bellowing Ark, 2009).

Jack D. Harvey's poetry has appeared in *Scrivener, The Comstock Review, Valparaiso Poetry Review, Typishly Literary Magazine, The Antioch Review, The Piedmont Poetry Journal*, and elsewhere. The author has been a Pushcart nominee and over the years has been published in a few anthologies.

Shaun Haurin is the author of *Public Displays of Affectation*, a story collection. His fiction has appeared in *New Ohio Review, Valparaiso*

Fiction Review, and *The Baltimore Review*, among other places. He lives in Greenwich, Connecticut.

Robin Herzog is a Swedish writer whose short stories belong to literary fiction, they are often set in the style of magical realism. He lives in Stockholm, Sweden, and has a BA degree in Journalism from Södertörn University. Robin is currently writing a short story collection.

Jim Jas was born and raised in Stockholm, Sweden, where he works as a software engineer. Jim studied poetry and fiction writing at the University of Sheffield, and he earned a bachelor in English from Stockholm University. Jim's work was nominated for the 2024 Pushcart Prize, and it has been featured in *Kelp*, *Literary Orphans*, *New Reader Magazine*, among others.

Rich Kenefic is a retired engineer living in the Midwest. His poems and essays can be found in recent or forthcoming issues of *Notre Dame Review*, *Tar River Poetry*, and the *Arkansas International*.

Susanna Lang divides her time between Chicago and Uzès, France. The 2024 winner of the Marvin Bell Memorial Poetry Prize from *December Magazine*, her most recent chapbook, *Like This*, was released in 2023 (Unsolicited Books), along with her translations of poems by Souad Labbize, *My Soul Has No Corners* (Diálogos Books). A new collection of Souad Labbize's poems, *Unfasten the Silk of Your Silence* is now available from Éditions des Lisières. Her third full-length collection of poems, *Travel Notes from the River Styx*, was published in 2017 by Terrapin Books. Her poems, translations, and reviews have appeared in such publications as *The Common*, *Asymptote*, *Tupelo*

Quarterly, American Life in Poetry, Rhino Reviews, Mayday, and *The Slowdown.* Her translations of poetry by Yves Bonnefoy include *Words in Stone* and *The Origin of Language,* and she is now working with Hélène Dorion and Christine Guinard on new translations.

Eric le Fatte was educated at MIT and Northeastern University in biology and English. He has worked correcting catalog cards in Texas, and as the Returns King at Eastern Mountain Sports, but currently hikes, writes, teaches, and does research on tiny things in the Portland, Oregon area. He has published poems in *Rune, The Mountain Gazette, The Poeming Pigeon, The Raven Chronicles, Windfall, Verseweavers, US#1 Worksheets, Perceptions, Cirque, Clade Song, Clover, Tiny Seed, Deep Wild, Canary,* and happily enough, in *The Clackamas Literary Review.*

Christine Marie raised two sons and worked as a secretary, counselor, and priest in Alaska, and is now retired and writing in a tower in Eugene, Oregon. Her poetry has been published in *The Sun, Timberline Review,* and other journals, and a chapbook for Alaska libraries, *Song for a Mountain.*

Judith Mikesch-McKenzie is a writer, teacher, actor, and producer. She holds a Masters in Creative Writing, and has years of experience teaching college writing. She has traveled widely, but is always drawn to the Rocky Mountains as one place that feeds her soul. Writing is her home. Her poetry has appeared in or is upcoming in *Calyx—A Journal of Art and Literature by Women, Her Words, Plainsongs Magazine, Hole In the Head Review, The Clackamas Literary Review,* and over 40 others.

Daniel Edward Moore lives in Washington on Whidbey Island. His work is forthcoming in *Drunk Monkeys, Xavier Review, The Chiron Review, Hurricane Review, Bryant Literary Review, The Meadow Journal,* and *The Stillwater Review.* His book, *Waxing the Dents,* is from Brick Road Poetry Press.

Daniel Thomas Moran, born in New York City in 1957, is the author of seventeen collections of poetry. *In the Kingdom of Autumn,* was published by Salmon Poetry in Ireland in 2020, who also published his previous collection, *A Shed for Wood* in 2014. His *Looking for the Uncertain Past* was published by Poetry Salzburg in 2005. His new collection, *Five Questions,* will be published by Salmon Poetry in early 2026. He has had more than four hundred poems published in more than twenty different countries. In 2005, he was appointed poet laureate by The Legislature of Suffolk County, New York. His collected papers are being archived by The Dept. of Special Collections at Stony Brook University. He is a retired Clinical Assistant Professor from Boston University's School of Dental Medicine, where he delivered the Commencement Address in 2011. He is Arts Editor for *The Humanist* magazine in Washington, DC. He and his wife Karen live in New Hampshire.

Cecil Morris, a retired high school English teacher and Pushcart and Best of the Net nominee, has poems appearing in *The Ekphrastic Review, Hole in the Head Review, Lascaux Review, New Verse News, Rust + Moth, Sugar House Review, Willawaw Journal,* and elsewhere. His debut poetry collection, *At Work in the Garden of Possibilities,* will come out from *Main Street Rag* in 2025.

Sharon Morris lives in Oregon with her husband John and her dog Pearl. She holds an MA and PhD from the University of Chicago and a BA from Mills College.

Bruce Parker has published two chapbooks, *Ramadan in Summer*, (Finishing Line Press, 2022) and *Tears for Things* (Plan B Press, 2024). He holds a BA in History from the University of Maryland, Far East Division, Okinawa, Japan, and an MA in Secondary Education from the University of New Mexico. His work appears or is forthcoming in *Triggerfish Critical Review*, *The Field Guide*, *Wild Roof*, *Cerasus* (UK), *The Brussels Review* (Belgium), and *Prairie Schooner*. Married to fellow poet and artist Diane Corson, he lives in Portland, Oregon, where they host a monthly poetry critique workshop, "Portland Ars Poetica." He is past president of the Oregon Poetry Association and a former Assistant Editor at Boulevard.

Vivienne Popperl's poems have appeared in *The Clackamas Literary Review*, *Timberline Review*, *About Place Journal*, *One Art*, and other publications. She received several awards from Willamette Writers and the Oregon Poetry Association. Her first collection, *A Nest in the Heart*, was published by The Poetry Box in April, 2022. A transplant from the Southern Hemisphere, she now revels in the moody fog and mist of the Pacific Northwest.

samodH Porawagamage is the author of *becoming sam* (Burnside Review Press) and *All the Salty Sand in Our Mouths* (forthcoming from Airlie Press). His writing focuses on the Sri Lankan Civil War, poverty and underdevelopment, colonial and imperial atrocities, and disproportionate impacts of climate change on rural and marginalized communities.

Richard Robbins was raised in California and Montana, taught for many years in Minnesota, and recently moved back west to Oregon. He studied poetry writing with Richard Hugo and Madeline DeFrees at the University of Montana. Lynx House Press recently published his seventh book, *The Oratory of All Souls*.

Now that **Patrick S. Rogers** operates a truck scale at a non-ferrous metal recycler in Portland, Oregon, his Poetry MFA in Creative Writing from Portland State gives him imposter syndrome until a lit mag like *Propeller Magazine* or *The Clackamas Literary Review* decides to accept one of his poems. His wife Wendy Bourgeois, also a poet, assures him his 2 Boston Terriers, Chico Party and Dot-Dot, don't care about the truck scale or the MFA.

Bradley Samore has worked as an editor, writing consultant, English teacher, creative writing teacher, basketball coach, and family support facilitator. His writing has appeared in *The Florida Review*, *Carve*, *The Dewdrop*, and other publications. He was named a Joint Winner of the Creative Writing Ink Poetry Prize.

David Sapp, writer and artist, lives along the southern shore of Lake Erie in North America. A Pushcart nominee, he was awarded Ohio Arts Council Individual Excellence Grants for poetry and the visual arts. His poetry and prose appear widely in the United States, Canada, and the United Kingdom. His publications include articles in the *Journal of Creative Behavior*, chapbooks *Close to Home* and *Two Buddha*, a novel *Flying Over Erie*, and a book of poems and drawings titled *Drawing Nirvana*.

Shawn Schenck (he/him) is an author, musician, and horror writer for The Game of Nerds. His writing includes elements of horror, the weird, crime, and fabulism. Shawn's work has been featured in *The Clackamas Literary Review*, *Wingless Dreamer's Midnight Masquerade*, and The Yard: Crime Blog. He enjoys reading and watching films with his fiancé and son, and his favorite color is yellow.

Eric W. Schramm lives in Ann Arbor, Michigan, and works for the University of Michigan. His poems have appeared in *Great Lakes Review*, *Passenger Journal*, *Gargoyle*, *The Literary Review*, *New Zoo Poetry Review*, *The Potomac*, *The Louisville Review*, and *Gyroscope Review*, among others.

Bill Schreiber has been a Hyla Brook Poet since 2018. Bill has been published in *Aerial Perspective*, *Assignment Literary Magazine*, *Broadkill Review*, *Gyroscope Review*, *Shot Glass Journal*, *The Poets Touchstone,* and *Metonym Journal*. Bill works in the technology field and lives with his wife and son in southern New Hampshire.

Erik Manuel Soto is a Mexican-American writer from California. His poems have appeared in *Volt*, *The Nelligan*, *River and South Review*, *Huizache*, and *Sonora Review*. Winner of the inaugural Gronk Nicandro first book prize for poetry, Erik debuts his full-length poetry collection, *Inside the Umber Iris*. He is currently bouncing around the West Coast.

Sam Spring is best known for his songwriting work in the musical duo Tennis Club with their song, "Morning," eclipsing 6,000,000 plays on Spotify alone. The 28-year-old has poetry and short fiction appearing in *Passengers Journal, The Wisconsin Review, Denver Quarterly*, and *The Clackamas Literary Review* among others.

Geo. Staley is retired from teaching writing and literature at Portland Community College. He had also taught in New England, Appalachia, and on the Rosebud Sioux Indian Reservation. His poetry has appeared in *Freshwater, Main Street Rag, The Clackamas Literary Review, Naugatuck River Review, Willow Review, Trajectory, Evening Street Review, Paddock Review, Slab, Book of Matches, Slipstream, Change Seven*, and others.

Ahrend Torrey is the author of *This Moment* (Pinyon Publishing, 2024); *If it's darkness we're having, let it be extravagant: The Jane Kenyon Erasure Poems* (Pinyon Publishing, 2024); *For What Are the Blossoms Reaching?* (Limited Artist's Edition, American Academy of Bookbinding, 2023); *Ripples* (Pinyon Publishing, 2023); *Bird City, American Eye* (Pinyon Publishing, 2022); and *Small Blue Harbor* (Poetry Box Select, 2019). His work has appeared in *Denver Quarterly, storySouth, The Greensboro Review, The Westchester Review, Welter*, and *West Trade Review*, among others. He lives in Chicago with his husband, Jonathan; their two rat terriers, Dichter and Dova; and Purl, their cat.

Phil Wetjen's fiction has appeared in *The Clackamas Literary Review*. His non-fiction work was published as a Commentary in the journal *Critical Asian Studies*. He studied Economics at Binghamton University and recently published his first novel.

Jonathan Wlodarski is a graduate of the PhD in creative writing program at the University of Nebraska–Lincoln. His work has appeared in *Ninth Letter, Foglifter Journal,* and *Barely South Review,* and his chapbook *Recipes for Grief* is forthcoming from Abode Press.

Ty Zhang (he/him) is a Thai-American law student, writer, and political organizer based in Ohio. He writes poetry, prose, and screenplays. His work has recently appeared in *Assignment Literary Magazine, BarBar Literary Magazine,* and *Meniscus.*

The *Clackamas Literary Review* is typeset in Sabon LT Std, an oldstyle serif designed by Jan Tschichold, and in Optima, a humanistic sans-serif designed by Hermann Zapf, and printed on 50 lb. creme paper. Editing and design done by English Department students and faculty at Clackamas Community College, in Oregon City, Oregon.

Visit

CLR

CLACKAMAS LITERARY REVIEW

clackamasliteraryreview.wordpress.com
clackamasliteraryreview.submittable.com
facebook.com/clackamasliteraryreview
@clackamaslitrev

Contact
clr@clackamas.edu

CLACKAMAS LITERARY REVIEW

the finest writing for the best readers

Clackamas Literary Review has been committed to publishing quality writing from around the world since 1997. Use the form below or visit us on Submittable to receive the latest and forthcoming issues.

Clackamas Literary Review

_____	1 year	$15
_____	2 years	$28
_____	3 years	$40

Name _____

Address _____

City / State / Zip _____

Email _____

Send this form and check or money order to:

Clackamas Literary Review
English Department
Clackamas Community College
19600 Molalla Avenue
Oregon City, Oregon 97045
